序　言

　　教育部專款補助「財團法人語言訓練測驗中心」，推行「全民英語能力分級檢定測驗」後，預計在未來，所有國小、國中學生，以及一般社會人士，如計程車駕駛、百貨業、餐飲業、旅遊業或觀光景點服務人員、維修技術人員、一般行政助理等，均須通過「初級英語能力檢定測驗」，以作為畢業、就業、升遷時之英語能力證明，已是必然趨勢，此項測驗的重要性，可見一斑。

　　本書編者林銀姿老師實際參加考試，了解出題方向，推出「初級英檢模擬試題①②」後，我們再推出「初級英檢模擬試題③」，完全仿照「初級英語能力檢定測驗」中的題型，書中囊括聽力測驗、閱讀能力測驗，以及寫作能力測驗，希望能幫助讀者輕鬆通過初級檢定的初試測驗。本書試題全部經過劉毅英文「初級英語檢定模考班」，實際在課堂上使用過，效果奇佳。本書所有試題均附有詳細的中文翻譯及單字註解，節省讀者查字典的時間。同時，這些珍貴的試題，也有助於國中同學準備基本學力測驗及第二階段考試。

　　感謝這麼多讀者，給我們鼓勵。編輯好書，是「學習」一貫的宗旨，讀者若需要任何學習英文的書，都可以提供意見給我們，我們的目標是，學英文的書，「學習」都有；「學習」出版、天天進步。也盼望讀者們不吝給我們批評指正。

編者　謹識

本書製作過程

　　感謝劉毅英文「初級英語檢定模考班」的同學們，在上課的八週期間，提供許多寶貴的意見，讓這些試題更加完善。感謝美籍老師 Laura E. Stewart 負責校訂，也要感謝謝靜芳老師再三仔細校訂，白雪嬌小姐負責封面設計，李佩姍小姐繪製插圖，洪淑娟小姐協助完稿，黃淑貞小姐負責版面設計，蘇淑玲小姐協助打字。

全民英語能力分級檢定測驗
初級測驗①

一、聽力測驗

　　本測驗分三部份，全為三選一之選擇題，每部份各 10 題，共 30 題，作答時間約 20 分鐘。

第一部份：看圖辨義

　　本部份共 10 題，試題冊上每題有一個圖片，請聽錄音機播出一個相關的問題，與 A、B、C 三個英語敘述後，選一個與所看到圖片最相符的答案，並在答案紙上相對的圓圈內塗黑作答。每題播出一遍，問題及選項均不印在試題冊上。

例：（看）

NT$80　　**NT$50**

（聽）

Look at the picture. How much is the hamburger?

　　A. It's eighty dollars.
　　B. It's fifty-five dollars.
　　C. It's eighteen dollars.

正確答案為 A

Question 1

Question 2

Question 3

Question 4

Question 5

Question 6

請 翻 頁 ⟹

Question 7

Question 8

Question 9

Question 10

請 翻 頁 ▯▯⟹

第二部份：問答

本部份共 10 題，每題錄音機會播出一個問句或直述句，
每題播出一次，聽後請從試題冊上 A、B、C 三個選項中，
選出一個最適合的回答或回應，並在答案紙上塗黑作答。

例：

（聽）　Good morning, Kevin.　How are you?

（看）　A.　I'm fine, thank you.
　　　　B.　I'm in the living room.
　　　　C.　My name is Kevin.

正確答案為 A

11. A. His name is Fred.
　　B. Speaking.
　　C. No, he's out.

13. A. I don't need glasses.
　　B. They're on the table.
　　C. I'll see them later.

12. A. Yes, it was wonderful.
　　B. I'll have a number
　　　 two meal.
　　C. No, thank you.　I'm
　　　 not hungry now.

14. A. It has two bedrooms.
　　B. It's 25,000 per
　　　 month.
　　C. It's on First Avenue.

15. A. No, it's Tuesday.
    B. Yes, it is.
    C. Have a nice day.

16. A. I usually play for an
       hour.
    B. I often play with my
       brother.
    C. Once or twice a week.

17. A. From Gate 13.
    B. At 12:30.
    C. On Tuesday.

18. A. Let's go to a movie.
    B. With my parents.
    C. I studied for the exam.

19. A. My mother drove me.
    B. About an hour ago.
    C. We're on Chunghsiao
       East Road.

20. A. No I can't. Can you?
    B. No problem.
    C. Help yourself.

請 翻 頁 ⫸

第三部份： 簡短對話

本部份共10題，每題錄音機會播出一段對話及一個相關的問題，每題播出兩次，聽後請從試題冊上A、B、C三個選項中，選出一個最適合的回答，並在答案紙上塗黑作答。

例：

(聽) (Woman)   Good afternoon, …Mr. Davis?

(Man)   Yes. I have an appointment with Dr. Sanders at two o'clock. My son Tommy has a fever.

(Woman)   Oh, that's too bad. Well, please have a seat, Mr. Davis. Dr. Sanders will be right with you.

Question: Where did this conversation take place?

(看) A. In a post office.

B. In a restaurant.

C. In a doctor's office.

正確答案為 C

21. A. At 11:00.
    B. In the afternoon.
    C. Tomorrow.

22. A. He will ride a
       bicycle.
    B. He will take a bus.
    C. He will take the
       MRT.

23. A. The man's question.
    B. The weather report.
    C. A music program.

24. A. 500 dollars.
    B. Three.
    C. Two and a half.

25. A. The man must move
       to a house near the
       park.
    B. The man probably
       lives close to the park.
    C. Only residents are
       allowed to use the
       park.

26. A. The boy will go to
       Japan with his
       grandmother.
    B. The boy will stay in
       Japan alone.
    C. The boy will visit his
       grandmother.

請 翻 頁 ⃞⇒

27. A. He can draw better than
       he can paint.
    B. He does not like to
       paint as much as he
       likes to draw.
    C. He can paint as well as
       the girl.

28. A. The woman does not
       like comedies or horror
       movies at all.
    B. The woman likes
       romances more than
       horror movies.
    C. The woman likes
       comedies as much as
       romances.

29. A. In a bakery.
    B. In a restaurant.
    C. In a party store.

30. A. The weather may
       be bad.
    B. He is not sure that
       he likes the beach.
    C. Going to the beach
       is never a good
       idea.

二、閱讀能力測驗

本測驗分三部份，全為四選一之選擇題，共 35 題，作答時間 35 分鐘。

第一部份：詞彙和結構

本部份共15題，每題含一個空格。請就試題冊上 A、B、C、D 四個選項中選出最適合題意的字或詞，標示在答案紙上。

1. It's almost 7:30. Get up quickly and _____ to school.
   A. arrive
   B. attend
   C. hurry
   D. follow

2. Tanya is eleven, and Becky is twelve. Tanya is _____ to Becky by one year.
   A. elementary
   B. junior
   C. senior
   D. similar

3. The speaker will allow students to _____ today's speech.
   A. record
   B. remember
   C. reach
   D. react

請 翻 頁 ▯▯⟹

4. You can learn more by _____ the new lesson before class.
   A. reviewing
   B. concentrating
   C. previewing
   D. focusing

5. The _____ doesn't work, so the room is hot and stuffy.
   A. cell phone
   B. air conditioner
   C. washing machine
   D. vending machine

6. When the final exam was over, my sister and I rode our bikes home. We went to bed right away because _____ of us were very tired.
   A. all
   B. three
   C. most
   D. both

7. Studying with good friends _____ fun.
   A. is a lot of
   B. are great
   C. has much
   D. have a lot of

8. Alice _____ the English composition since this morning.
   A. will write
   B. has been writing
   C. would write
   D. writes

9. Sarah invited _____ to celebrate her fourteenth birthday
   in a Japanese restaurant.
   A. we
   B. our
   C. ours
   D. us

10. If you want to have a lot of friends, avoid _____ other
    people.
    A. to criticize
    B. criticizing
    C. criticize
    D. to criticizing

11. When I heard the bad news, I was so shocked _____
    I couldn't speak a word.
    A. than
    B. to
    C. too
    D. that

請翻頁 ⟹

12. My pencil box is yellow. _____ is blue.
    A. Her
    B. My
    C. His
    D. Our

13. What's going _____ here? Why are you so upset?
    A. in
    B. with
    C. up
    D. on

14. My father has me _____ the living room.
    A. to vacuum
    B. vacuum
    C. vacuumed
    D. vacuuming

15. Would you mind _____ this note to Frank?
    A. giving
    B. to giving
    C. to give
    D. give

第二部份：段落填空

　　　　本部份共 10 題，包括二個段落，每個段落各含 5 個空格。
　　　　請就試題冊上 A、B、C、D 四個選項中選出最適合題意
　　　　的字或詞，標示在答案紙上。

Questions 16-20

　　Wouldn't it be "cool" to take a ___(16)___ at a hotel which was ___(17)___ ice? Well, at Sweden's ice hotel, even the beds are made of ice! So, spending a night there ___(18)___ that you need to wear a lot of clothes. A Swede called Yngve Bergqvist built the hotel. The hotel is near the Arctic Circle. It has more than 60 rooms and its own ice church. More than 8,000 people ___(19)___ the hotel every year. Every spring the hotel melts away, and every fall it has to ___(20)___ all over again.

16. A. class
    B. lesson
    C. medicine
    D. vacation

17. A. made of
    B. made by
    C. build of
    D. build by

18. A. mean
    B. means
    C. is meant
    D. are meant

19. A. visit
    B. tell
    C. return
    D. ring

20. A. build
    B. built
    C. is built
    D. be built

請 翻 頁 ◁══▷

Questions 21-25

Albert is going to enter the race on his school's ___(21)___ day. For that reason, he practices a lot every day. In the morning, he goes swimming for one hour, jogging for one hour, and ___(22)___ for two hours. He also drinks a lot of water and eats foods which are good ___(23)___ his health. He likes ___(24)___, potato chips and ice cream. But now he has to stop ___(25)___ such food because he wants to do his best in the race.

21. A. sports
    B. birth
    C. running
    D. singing

22. A. eating
    B. reading
    C. sleeping
    D. cycling

23. A. for
    B. with
    C. in
    D. at

24. A. fruit
    B. fries
    C. fish
    D. vegetables

25. A. to eat
    B. to eating
    C. and eat
    D. eating

第三部份： 閱讀理解

本部份共 10 題，包括數段短文，每段短文後有 1～3 個相關問題，請就試題冊上 A、B、C、D 四個選項中選出最適合者，標示在答案紙上。

Question 26

26. What does this sign mean?

A. No fishing.

B. No smoking.

C. No parking.

D. No barbecuing.

請翻頁 ◄▭▭⟹

Questions 27-28

Part-Time Tutor Wanted

➡ University graduate

➡ Good command of English

➡ Work from 7:30 p.m. to 8:30 p.m. every

  Monday and Wednesday

➡ Near Wanfang Hospital Station

  Telephone: (02) 2723-5678   Miss Wu

---

27. Who is looking for a tutor?
    A. A university graduate.
    B. A man living near Wanfang Hospital Station.
    C. A person who speaks English.
    D. Miss Wu.

28. Who will **NOT** get the job?
    A. People who are not from the U.S.
    B. People who are not free in the evening on Wednesdays.
    C. People who are fluent in English.
    D. People who work in Wanfang Hospital.

Questions 29-30

★ *Daily Service* ★

🚌 Tickets 🚌

↑ One way—$16.00   ↓↑ Round trip— $30.00

Burly to Monty		Monty to Burly	
Leaves Burly	Arrives Monty	Leaves Monty	Arrives Burly
6:30 am	8:30 am	9:00 am	11:00 am
11:30 am	1:30 pm	2:00 pm	4:00 pm
4:30 am	6:30 am	7:00 pm	9:00 pm

29. If you arrive in Monty at 8:30 am and spend all day there with a friend, when does the last bus you can take home to Burly leave?
   A. 2:00 pm.   B. 4:00 pm.
   C. 7:00 pm.   D. 9:00 pm.

30. Which of the following is true?
   A. There are two morning trips from Monty to Burly.
   B. A round-trip ticket from Burly to Monty is $32.00.
   C. The 11:30 am bus arrives in Monty at 2:00 pm.
   D. The bus trip from Burly to Monty is two hours.

請 翻 頁 ◀▭⟩

Questions 31-32

A

B

I've been here in Waterfield for two months. Ben and I spent the Easter vacation on Ben's uncle's farm.

Every morning his uncle drove us to a lake. We fished there. Ben could not catch any fish, but I caught four big ones on the last day. We cooked the fish on a barbecue, and had them for lunch. They tasted wonderful!

In the afternoon we worked very hard on the farm. We wanted to help his uncle. The work on the farm was not as easy as I thought, but it was interesting. Together with the letter are some pictures we took. They are beautiful, aren't they?

C

D

31. If this letter was written on January 5, the photos
    mentioned in the letter probably
    A. were taken on New Year's Day.
    B. were taken by Ben's uncle.
    C. will be taken on January 25.
    D. will be sent next time.

32. What should be filled in ____C____?
    A. Dear Nora,
    B. January 5
    C. Jacky
    D. Sincerely,

Questions 33-35

Some people might say that driving a bus is a boring job. I don't think so. Every day, I can meet people I have never seen before. I enjoy talking to them. And more importantly, I know that without me, many of them could not get to work or school. Helping people in this way gives me a good feeling. Even if there is nobody on my bus, I can watch small changes along the way. That green tree has gotten taller; the man in the red house has grown more flowers in front of his house. These are the things that make me feel satisfied.

33. What is the writer?
    A. A bus driver.
    B. A taxi driver.
    C. A policeman.
    D. A mechanic.

34. What is the most important thing that the writer likes about his work?

   A. He can meet different kinds of people.

   B. He can keep the change.

   C. He can help people.

   D. He can talk to people.

35. Which is true?

   A. The writer feels sad when there is nobody on the bus.

   B. The writer wants to change his job.

   C. The writer can notice some small changes along the way.

   D. The writer doesn't feel comfortable on the bus.

請 翻 頁 ◖◼⇒

三、寫作能力測驗

　　本測驗共有兩部份，第一部份為單句寫作，第二部份為段落寫作。測驗時間為 40 分鐘。

第一部份：單句寫作

　　　　請將答案寫在寫作能力測驗答案紙對應的題號旁，如有拼字、標點、大小寫之錯誤，將予扣分。

第 1～5 題：句子改寫

　　　　請依題目之提示，將原句改寫成指定型式，並將改寫的句子完整地寫在答案紙上（包括提示之文字及標點符號）。

1. I asked Tina, "Could you open the window?"
   I asked Tina whether _____.

2. Sally is shorter than all the other students in her class.
   Sally _____ shortest _____ in her class.

3. Tim didn't go to school because he didn't feel well.
   Tim _____, so _____.

4. Jane didn't hand in her report on time.
   Why _____?

5. Our teacher made this cake.
   This cake _____ our teacher.

第 6～10 題：句子合併

請依照題目指示，將兩句合併成一句，並將合併的句子
完整地寫在答案紙上（包括提示之文字及標點符號）。

6. Kevin has a backpack.
   The backpack is black.

   Kevin _____ _____ backpack.

7. Where are they going to?
   I'd like to know.

   I'd like to know where _____.

8. Little Wendy can't sleep.
   She needs to hold her blanket.

   Little Wendy _____ without _____.

9. I have a computer.
   My computer is new and expensive.

   I have _____ which _____.

10. My mother is here.
    My father is here, too.

    Both _____ and _____.

請翻頁 ⟹

第 11～15 題：重組

請將題目中所有提示字詞整合成一有意義的句子，並將重組的句子完整地寫在答案紙上（包括提示之文字及標點符號）。答案中必須使用所有提示字詞，且不能隨意增加字詞，否則不予計分。

11. Peter _____.

understanding / what / has / the child / is saying / trouble

12. I _____.

get up / in / at / used to / the morning / five o'clock

13. Keep _____!

or / get / quiet / out

14. James _____.

looking for / for / a / house / has / a while / new / been

15. Gary _____.

as long as / is not / will / raining / jog / it

第二部份：段落寫作

題目：現在正是暑假時期，下面是你每天的活動，請根據這些圖片
　　　寫一篇約 50 字的簡短描述。

初級英檢模擬試題① 詳解

一、聽力測驗

第一部份

Look at the picture for question 1.

1. (**C**) What can the girl see in the window?

　　A. A baby.　　　B. A duck.

　　C. A doll.

　　* window〔'wɪndo〕*n.* 窗戶；（商店的）櫥窗
　　　duck〔dʌk〕*n.* 鴨子　　doll〔dɑl〕*n.* 洋娃娃；玩偶

Look at the picture for question 2.

2. (**C**) What is the police officer doing?

　　A. He is driving.　　B. He is dancing.

　　C. He is writing.

　　* *police officer* 警察　　drive〔draɪv〕*v.* 開車
　　　dance〔dæns〕*v.* 跳舞

Look at the picture for question 3.

3. (**B**) How does the boy feel?

　　A. It is broken.

　　B. He is nervous.

　　C. He threw the ball.

　　* broken〔'brokən〕*adj.* 破碎的；故障的
　　　nervous〔'nɝvəs〕*adj.* 緊張的
　　　throw〔θro〕*v.* 投（三態變化為：throw-threw-thrown）

Look at the picture for question 4.

4. (**C**) What is the man doing?

    A. He is watering the flowers.

    B. He is taking a shower.

    C. He is washing the dog.

    * water (ˈwɔtɚ) v. 澆水

    take a shower 淋浴   wash (wɑʃ) v. 洗

Look at the picture for question 5.

5. (**C**) What did he find?

    A. He found the school.

    B. He dropped it.

    C. A wallet.

    * drop (drɑp) v. 使掉落

    wallet (ˈwɑlɪt) n. 皮夾

Look at the picture for question 6.

6. (**A**) What is he doing?

    A. He is fixing the toilet.

    B. He is in the bathroom.

    C. He is cleaning.

    * fix (fɪks) v. 修理   toilet (ˈtɔɪlɪt) n. 馬桶

    bathroom (ˈbæθ,rum) n. 洗手間；浴室

    clean (klin) v. 打掃

Look at the picture for question 7.

7. (**B**) How many children are watching the man?

    A. They are interested.

    B. There are five.

    C. He is happy.

    * interested〔'ɪntrɪstɪd〕adj. (人) 感興趣的

Look at the picture for question 8.

8. (**C**) Why is she closing the window?

    A. She is not tall enough.

    B. She wants to play outside.

    C. It is raining.

    * close〔kloz〕v. 關   tall〔tɔl〕adj. 高的
      outside〔'aʊt'saɪd〕adv. 在外面

Look at the picture for question 9.

9. (**B**) What is wrong with the bike?

    A. He is late for school.

    B. It has a flat tire.

    C. It is very tired.

    * *What is wrong with~?* ~怎麼了？
      (= *What is the matter with~?*)
      bike〔baɪk〕n. 腳踏車 (= *bicycle*)
      late〔let〕adj. 遲到的   flat〔flæt〕adj. (輪胎) 洩氣的
      tire〔taɪr〕n. 輪胎   *flat tire* 爆胎
      tired〔taɪrd〕adj. 疲倦的

Look at the picture for question 10.

10. (**C**) What are they watching?

    A. Pizza.

    B. In a theater.

    C. A movie.

    * pizza (ˈpitsə) *n.* 披薩

      theater (ˈθiətɚ) *n.* 戲院；電影院

      movie (ˈmuvɪ) *n.* 電影

第二部份

11. (**C**) Hello, Jane. Is your father there?

    A. His name is Fred.

    B. Speaking.

    C. No, he's out.

    * **Speaking**. （電話用語）我就是。

      out (aut) *adv.* 外出

12. (**A**) Did you enjoy your meal?

    A. Yes, it was wonderful.

    B. I'll have a number two meal.

    C. No, thank you. I'm not hungry now.

    * meal (mil) *n.* 一餐

      wonderful (ˈwʌndɚfəl) *adj.* 很棒的   have (hæv) *v.* 吃

      number (ˈnʌmbɚ) *n.* 號碼；編號

      hungry (ˈhʌŋgrɪ) *adj.* 飢餓的

13. (**B**) Have you seen my glasses?

    A. I don't need glasses.

    B. They're on the table.

    C. I'll see them later.

    * glasses〔'glæsɪz〕*n. pl.* 眼鏡   later〔'letɚ〕*adv.* 稍後

14. (**B**) How much is the apartment?

    A. It has two bedrooms.

    B. It's 25,000 per month.

    C. It's on First Avenue.

    * apartment〔ə'pɑrtmənt〕*n.* 公寓
    bedroom〔'bɛd,rum〕*n.* 臥室   per〔pɝ〕*prep.* 每
    month〔mʌnθ〕*n.* 月   avenue〔'ævə,nju〕*n.* 大街

15. (**B**) Good morning, Patrick. Nice day, isn't it?

    A. No, it's Tuesday.

    B. Yes, it is.

    C. Have a nice day.

    * nice〔naɪs〕*adj.* 好的；令人愉快的

16. (**C**) How often do you play tennis?

    A. I usually play for an hour.

    B. I often play with my brother.

    C. Once or twice a week.

    * *How often~?* ~多久一次？   tennis〔'tɛnɪs〕*n.* 網球
    once〔wʌns〕*adv.* 一次   twice〔twaɪs〕*adv.* 兩次

17. (**B**) What time does the flight leave?

    A. From Gate 13.

    B. At 12:30.

    C. On Tuesday.

    * flight〔flaɪt〕*n.* 班機   leave〔liv〕*v.* 離開
      gate〔get〕*n.* 登機門

18. (**C**) What did you do last night?

    A. Let's go to a movie.

    B. With my parents.

    C. I studied for the exam.

    * ***go to a movie*** 去看電影   exam〔ɪg'zæm〕*n.* 考試

19. (**A**) How did you get here?

    A. My mother drove me.

    B. About an hour ago.

    C. We're on Chunghsiao East Road.

    * drive〔draɪv〕*v.* 開車載（某人）
      Chunghsiao East Road 忠孝東路

20. (**B**) Can you help me with this?

    A. No I can't. Can you?

    B. No problem.

    C. Help yourself.

    * ***help*** sb. ***with*** sth. 幫忙某人做某事
      No problem. 沒問題。
      help oneself 自行取用

第三部份

21. (**B**) M : What time is your next class?

W : Not until 11:00.

M : Mine, too. How about getting a cup of coffee?

W : Good idea. We can talk about the history homework.

M : Yeah. We have to hand it in in class this afternoon.

Question : When do they have the history class?

A. At 11:00.　　　　　B. In the afternoon.

C. Tomorrow.

* until〔ən'tɪl〕*prep.* 直到　　***not until*** ~　直到~才…

How about* ~ *?　~好嗎？（提出建議）　　get〔gɛt〕*v.* 買

coffee〔'kɔfɪ〕*n.* 咖啡　　***talk about*** 談論

history〔'hɪstrɪ〕*n.* 歷史　　***hand in*** 繳交

22. (**C**) M : Can you tell me the way to the zoo?

W : Sure. You just take the MRT to the last stop.

M : Do I have to take a bus from there?

W : No, you can walk from the station.

Question : How will the boy get to the zoo?

A. He will ride a bicycle.

B. He will take a bus.

C. He will take the MRT.

* zoo〔zu〕*n.* 動物園

MRT 捷運（ = *Mass Rapid Transit*）

the last stop 最後一站　　station〔'steʃən〕*n.* 車站

get to 到達　　ride〔raɪd〕*v.* 騎

23. (**B**) M: Did you listen to the forecast?

W: Yes, I listened to the report on the radio.

M: What did it say?

W: It will be cold tomorrow, but sunny.

Question: What did the woman listen to on the radio?

A. The man's question.

B. The weather report.

C. A music program.

* **listen to** 收聽　　forecast ('for,kæst) n. (天氣) 預報
report (rɪ'port) n. 報導
radio ('redɪ,o) n. 收音機；廣播
sunny ('sʌnɪ) adj. 晴朗的　　**weather report** 氣象報導
program ('progræm) n. 節目

24. (**B**) W: Excuse me, how much are the tickets for the next show?

M: 200 dollars for adults; half price for children and seniors.

W: Two adults and one child, please.

Question: How many people will go to the show?

A. 500 dollars.

B. Three.

C. Two and a half.

* ticket ('tɪkɪt) n. 入場券　　show (ʃo) n. 表演
adult (ə'dʌlt) n. 成人　　half (hæf) adj. 一半的　n. 一半
senior ('sinjɚ) n. 年長者　　child (tʃaɪld) n. 小孩

25. (**B**) W: Do you often come to this park?

M: Yes. I come every morning.

W: Oh. You must live nearby.

Question: What does the woman mean?

A. The man must move to a house near the park.

B. The man probably lives close to the park.

C. Only residents are allowed to use the park.

* must〔mʌst〕*aux.* 一定；必須
nearby〔'nɪr'baɪ〕*adv.* 在附近　　move〔muv〕*v.* 搬家
probably〔'prɑbəblɪ〕*adv.* 可能　　***close to*** 接近
resident〔'rɛzədənt〕*n.* 居民　　allow〔ə'laʊ〕*v.* 允許

26. (**C**) W: Where are your parents going?

M: They are going to Japan for a vacation.

W: Will you stay here alone?

M: No. I'm going to stay with my grandmother
for a week.

Question: Which of the following is true?

A. The boy will go to Japan with his grandmother.

B. The boy will stay in Japan alone.

C. The boy will visit his grandmother.

* Japan〔dʒə'pæn〕*n.* 日本
vacation〔ve'keʃən〕*n.* 假期
stay〔ste〕*v.* 停留；暫住　　alone〔ə'lon〕*adv.* 獨自地
grandmother〔'grænd,mʌðɚ〕*n.*（外）祖母
following〔'fɑləwɪŋ〕*adj.* 以下的
true〔tru〕*adj.* 眞實的；正確的　　visit〔'vɪzɪt〕*v.* 拜訪

27. (**A**)　W: You draw very well.

　　　　　M: Thank you.　I've been taking art lessons.

　　　　　W: Do you also paint?

　　　　　M: Yes, but not so well.

　　　　　Question: What does the boy mean?

　　　　　A. He can draw better than he can paint.

　　　　　B. He does not like to paint as much as he likes to draw.

　　　　　C. He can paint as well as the girl.

　　　　　* draw〔drɔ〕v. 畫畫（用鉛筆）　　*take lessons* 上課
　　　　　　art〔ɑrt〕n. 藝術　　paint〔pent〕v. 畫畫（用水彩）
　　　　　　as well as 和⋯ 一樣好

28. (**B**)　M: Do you prefer comedies or horror movies?

　　　　　W: They're both O.K.　But neither is my favorite.

　　　　　M: Oh?　What do you like most?

　　　　　W: I like romances.

　　　　　Question: Which of the following is true?

　　　　　A. The woman does not like comedies or horror movies
　　　　　　at all.

　　　　　B. The woman likes romances more than horror movies.

　　　　　C. The woman likes comedies as much as romances.

　　　　　* prefer〔prɪ'fɝ〕v. 比較喜歡
　　　　　　comedy〔'kɑmədɪ〕n. 喜劇　　*horror movie* 恐怖片
　　　　　　neither〔'niðɚ〕pron. 兩者皆不
　　　　　　favorite〔'fevərɪt〕n. 最喜歡的人或事物
　　　　　　romance〔ro'mæns〕n. 愛情故事
　　　　　　not⋯at all 一點也不

29. (**A**)　M：Can I help you?

　　　　W：Yes.　I'd like one loaf of that bread and two rolls.

　　　　M：Anything else?

　　　　W：Yes.　I want to order a birthday cake for tomorrow.

　　　　Question：Where did this conversation take place?

　　　　A. In a bakery.

　　　　B. In a restaurant.

　　　　C. In a party store.

　　　　* loaf〔lof〕 *n.* 一條（麵包）　　　bread〔brɛd〕 *n.* 麵包
　　　　　roll〔rol〕 *n.* 麵包捲　　order〔'ɔrdə〕 *v.* 訂購
　　　　　conversation〔ˌkɑnvə'seʃən〕 *n.* 對話
　　　　　take place 發生　　bakery〔'bekərɪ〕 *n.* 麵包店
　　　　　restaurant〔'rɛstərənt〕 *n.* 餐廳
　　　　　party store 派對用品專賣店

30. (**A**)　W：Would you like to go to the beach with us?

　　　　M：I'd like to, but I'm not sure it's a good idea.

　　　　W：Why?

　　　　M：It looks like rain.

　　　　Question：What does the boy mean?

　　　　A. The weather may be bad.

　　　　B. He is not sure that he likes the beach.

　　　　C. Going to the beach is never a good idea.

　　　　* beach〔bitʃ〕 *n.* 海灘　　sure〔ʃur〕 *adj.* 確定的
　　　　　It looks like rain. 看起來快下雨了。
　　　　　mean〔min〕 *v.* 意思是　　never〔'nɛvə〕 *adv.* 絕非

二、閱讀能力測驗

第一部份：詞彙和結構

1. (**C**) It's almost 7:30.　Get up quickly and <u>hurry</u> to school.
　　　　　現在已經快七點半了。快點起床，<u>趕快</u>到學校。

　　　　　(A) arrive〔ə'raɪv〕v. 到達
　　　　　(B) attend〔ə'tɛnd〕v. 上（學）
　　　　　(C) *hurry*〔'hɜɪ〕v. 趕快前往
　　　　　(D) follow〔'falo〕v. 跟隨
　　　　　* almost〔'ɔl,most〕adv. 幾乎　　*get up* 起床

2. (**B**) Tanya is eleven, and Becky is twelve.　Tanya is <u>junior</u> to Becky by one year.
　　　　　唐雅今年十一歲，貝姬今年十二歲。唐雅<u>比</u>貝姬<u>小</u>一歲。

　　　　　(A) elementary〔,ɛlə'mɛntərɪ〕adj. 基本的
　　　　　(B) *junior*〔'dʒunjɚ〕adj. 較…年輕的 < *to* >
　　　　　(C) senior〔'sinjɚ〕adj. 較…年長的 < *to* >
　　　　　(D) similar〔'sɪmələ〕adj. 相似的 < *to* >
　　　　　* by 表「差距」。

3. (**A**) The speaker will allow students to <u>record</u> today's speech.
　　　　　演說者將會允許學生<u>錄下</u>今天的演講。

　　　　　(A) *record*〔rɪ'kɔrd〕v. 錄音
　　　　　(B) remember〔rɪ'mɛmbɚ〕v. 記得
　　　　　(C) reach〔ritʃ〕v. 到達
　　　　　(D) react〔rɪ'ækt〕v. 反應
　　　　　* speaker〔'spikɚ〕n. 演說者　　allow〔ə'lau〕v. 允許
　　　　　speech〔spitʃ〕n. 演講

4. (**C**) You can learn more by <u>previewing</u> the new lesson before class. 你可以藉由上課前<u>預習</u>新課程，而學到更多。

 (A) review (rɪˋvju) v. 複習
 (B) concentrate (ˋkɑnsnˏtret) v. 專心於 < on >
 (C) *preview* (ˋpriˏvju) v. 預習
 (D) focus (ˋfokəs) v. 專心於 < on >
 * *by + V-ing* 藉由~（方法）

5. (**B**) The <u>air conditioner</u> doesn't work, so the room is hot and stuffy. <u>冷氣機</u>壞了，所以房間又熱又悶。

 (A) cell phone 手機
 (B) *air conditioner* 冷氣機
 (C) washing machine 洗衣機
 (D) vending machine 自動販賣機
 * work (wɝk) v. （機器）運轉
 stuffy (ˋstʌfɪ) adj. （房間）通風不良的

6. (**D**) When the final exam was over, my sister and I rode our bikes home. We went to bed right away because <u>both</u> of us were very tired.
期末考結束後，我姊姊跟我騎腳踏車回家。我們馬上上床睡覺，因為我們<u>兩個</u>都很累。

 「姊姊和我」共兩個人，故代名詞用 both「兩者」。(A) all 指「（三者以上的）全部」，(B) three「三人」，(C) most「大部分」，用法皆不合。
 * *final exam* 期末考 over (ˋovɚ) adv. 結束
 ride (raɪd) v. 騎 *right away* 馬上

7. (**A**) Studying with good friends <u>is a lot of</u> fun.
和好朋友一起唸書，<u>是很</u>快樂的事情。

$\begin{cases} sth. + \text{be 動詞} + fun & \text{某事很有趣} \\ sb. + \text{have} + fun & \text{某人玩得很愉快} \end{cases}$

(B) 須改爲 is great fun（動名詞當主詞，視爲單數）
(C) 須改爲 is much fun（主詞爲事物）

8. (**B**) Alice <u>has been writing</u> the English composition since this morning. 愛麗絲從今天早上起，就一直<u>在寫</u>這篇英文作文。

有介系詞 since（自從）的句子中，動詞時態用「現在完成式」或「現在完成進行式」，表示「從過去持續到現在的動作或狀態」，故選 (B) *has been writing*。

* composition〔͵kɑmpə'zɪʃən〕 *n.* 作文

9. (**D**) Sarah invites <u>us</u> to celebrate her fourteenth birthday in a Japanese restaurant.
莎拉邀請<u>我們</u>到一家日本餐廳，慶祝她十四歲的生日。

動詞之後應接受詞，故選 (D) *us*（爲 we 的受格）。而 (A) we 是主格，(B) our 是所有格，(C) ours 是所有格代名詞，用法皆不合。

* invite〔ɪn'vaɪt〕 *v.* 邀請　　celebrate〔'sɛlə͵bret〕 *v.* 慶祝
one's + 序數 + *birthday* 某人幾歲的生日
Japanese〔͵dʒæpə'niz〕 *adj.* 日本的

10. (**B**) If you want to have a lot of friends, avoid <u>criticizing</u> other people. 如果你想要有很多朋友，就要避免<u>批評</u>別人。

avoid + *V-ing* 避免

* criticize〔'krɪtə͵saɪz〕 *v.* 批評

11. (**D**)　When I heard the bad news, I was so shocked <u>that</u> I couldn't speak a word.

　　　　當我聽到那個壞消息時，太震驚了，<u>以致於</u>說不出話來。

　　　　so…that~　如此…以致於~

　　　　* news〔njuz〕*n.* 消息　　shocked〔ʃɑkt〕*adj.* 感到震驚的
　　　　word〔wɜd〕*n.* 字；話

12. (**C**)　My pencil box is yellow.　<u>His</u> is blue.

　　　　我的鉛筆盒是黃色的。<u>他的</u>是藍色的。

　　　　按照句意，空格要填入 His pencil box（他的鉛筆盒），
　　　　而所有格代名詞可代替先前提到的名詞，故選 (C) ***His***。
　　　　而 (A) 須改爲 Hers，(B) 須改爲 Mine，(D) 須改爲 Ours，
　　　　才能選。

　　　　* ***pencil box*** 鉛筆盒

13. (**D**)　What's going <u>on</u> here?　Why are you so upset?

　　　　這裡<u>發生</u>了什麼事？爲什麼你這麼不高興呢？

　　　　go on　發生（= *happen*）

　　　　* upset〔ʌpˊsɛt〕*adj.* 不高興的

14. (**B**)　My father has me <u>vacuum</u> the living room.

　　　　爸爸要我<u>用吸塵器打掃</u>客廳。

　　　　have + *sb.* + 原形 ***V.***　要某人做~

　　　　* vacuum〔ˊvækjʊəm〕*v.* 用吸塵器打掃
　　　　the living room 客廳

15. (**A**) Would you mind <u>giving</u> this note to Frank?

你介不介意把這張字條<u>交給</u>法蘭克？

mind + *V-ing* 介意

* note〔not〕*n.* 字條

第二部份：段落填空

Questions 16-20

Wouldn't it be "cool" to take a <u>vacation</u> at a hotel which
        16
was <u>made of</u> ice? Well, at Sweden's ice hotel, even the beds are
    17
made of ice! So, spending a night there <u>means</u> that you need to
                                    18
wear a lot of clothes. A Swede called Yngve Bergqvist built the
hotel. The hotel is near the Arctic Circle. It has more than 60
rooms and its own ice church. More than 8,000 people <u>visit</u> the
                                                19
hotel every year. Every spring the hotel melts away, and every
fall it has to <u>be built</u> all over again.
            20

到一家冰造的旅館度假，不是件很「涼快（酷）」的事情嗎？是這樣的，有家位於瑞典的冰造旅館，連床也是用冰打造而成的！所以在那裡過夜，意味著你必須穿很多衣服。一位名為英夫‧貝格夫司特的瑞典人蓋了這間旅館。這間旅館靠近北極圈。它擁有六十多間房間和自己的冰造教堂。每年有八千多人會來這家旅館住宿。每年到了春天，旅館就會融化，所以每年秋天都必須重新建造一次。

cool〔kul〕*adj.* 涼快的；很酷的

hotel〔ho'tɛl〕*n.* 旅館　　ice〔aɪs〕*n.* 冰

Sweden〔'swidən〕*n.* 瑞典　　spend〔spɛnd〕*v.* 度過

a lot of 許多的　　Swede〔swid〕*n.* 瑞典人

call〔kɔl〕*v.* 稱做

build〔bɪld〕*v.* 建造（三態變化為：build-built-built）

Artic Circle 北極圈　　church〔tʃɝtʃ〕*n.* 教堂

more than 超過　　*melt away* 融化

fall〔fɔl〕*n.* 秋天　　*(all) over again* 重新

16.（**D**）(A) class〔klæs〕*n.*（一節）課　(B) lesson〔'lɛsn̩〕*n.* 課程
　　　　(C) medicine〔'mɛdəsn̩〕*n.* 藥
　　　　(D) *vacation*〔ve'keʃən〕*n.* 假期　　*take a vacation* 度假

17.（**A**）*be made of* 由…製成
　　　　⎰ …a hotel which *was made of* ice…
　　　　⎱ ＝ …a hotel which *was built by* ice…

18.（**B**）動名詞片語 spending a night there 做主詞，須視為單數，且
　　　　依句意為主動，故選 (B) *means*。　mean〔min〕*v.* 意謂著

19.（**A**）(A) *visit*〔'vɪzɪt〕*v.* 住宿　　　　(B) tell〔tɛl〕*v.* 告訴
　　　　(C) return〔rɪ'tɝn〕*v.* 歸還
　　　　(D) ring〔rɪŋ〕*v.* 按（鈴）；打電話

20.（**D**）按照句意，旅館每年秋天就必須「被重蓋一次」，have to
　　　　後面須接原形動詞，且 build 的被動語態為 built，故選 (D)
　　　　be built。

Questions 21-25

Albert is going to enter the race on his school's <u>sports</u> day.
                                                    21
For that reason, he practices a lot every day. In the morning, he

goes swimming for one hour, jogging for one hour, and <u>cycling</u>
                                                            22
for two hours. He also drinks a lot of water and eats foods which

are good <u>for</u> his health. He likes <u>fries</u>, potato chips and ice cream.
          23   24
But now he has to stop <u>eating</u> such food because he wants to do
                        25
his best in the race.

艾伯特即將要參加學校運動會的賽跑。因此他每天都做很多練習。
早上他去游泳一個小時、慢跑一個小時，還有騎腳踏車兩個小時。他也
喝大量的水，並且吃對他的健康有益的食物。他喜歡薯條、洋芋片和冰
淇淋。但是現在他必須停止吃這些食物了，因為他想在賽跑時有最好的
表現。

> enter〔ˈɛntɚ〕v. 參加　　race〔res〕n. 賽跑
> reason〔ˈrizn〕n. 原因；理由　　practice〔ˈpræktɪs〕v. 練習
> swim〔swɪm〕v. 游泳　　jog〔dʒɑg〕v. 慢跑
> health〔hɛlθ〕n. 健康　　*potato chips* 洋芋片
> *ice cream* 冰淇淋　　*do one's best* 全力以赴；盡力

21. (**A**) *sports day* （學校）運動會

22. (**D**) 依句意，他早上運動，故空格應填和運動有關的名詞，故選
　　　　　　(D) *cycling*〔ˈsaɪklɪŋ〕n. 騎腳踏車。

23. (**A**) *be good for* 對…有益

　　　　　　而 (D) be good at「擅長」，則不合句意。

24. (**B**) 依句意，他喜歡高熱量的食品，故選 (B) *fries* 〔frɑɪz〕 *n. pl.*
　　　　　　薯條（＝*French fries*）。而 (A) fruit「水果」，(C) fish
　　　　　　「魚」，(D) vegetable「蔬菜」，則不合句意。

25. (**D**) $\begin{cases} \textbf{\textit{stop}} + \textbf{\textit{V-ing}} \text{ 停止} \\ \textbf{\textit{stop}} + \textbf{\textit{to V}}. \text{ 停下來，去做} \end{cases}$

第三部份：閱讀理解

Question 26

26. (**B**) 這個告示牌是什麼意思？

　　　　(A) 禁止釣魚。　　　　　　(B) 禁止抽煙。

　　　　(C) 禁止停車　　　　　　　(D) 禁止烤肉。

　　　　* sign〔saɪn〕*n.* 告示牌　　mean〔min〕*v.* 意思是
　　　　　fish〔fɪʃ〕*v.* 釣魚　　smoke〔smok〕*v.* 抽煙
　　　　　park〔pɑrk〕*v.* 停車　　barbecue〔ˋbɑrbɪˌkju〕*v.* 烤肉

Questions 27-28

```
┌─────────────────────────────────────┐
│                                     │
│           徵 兼 職 家 教               │
│                                     │
│   ➤ 大學畢業生                        │
│                                     │
│   ➤ 精通英文                          │
│                                     │
│   ➤ 工作時間：每個星期一及星期三晚上        │
│                                     │
│      七點半到八點半                     │
│                                     │
│   ➤ 靠近萬芳醫院站                      │
│                                     │
│      電話：(02) 2723-5678    吳小姐     │
│                                     │
└─────────────────────────────────────┘
```

part-time〔'pɑrt'taɪm〕adj. 兼職的
tutor〔'tjutɚ〕n. 家庭教師；私人教師
wanted〔'wɑntɪd〕adj. 徵…的
university〔,junə'vɝsətɪ〕n. 大學
graduate〔'grædʒuɪt〕n. 畢業生
command〔kə'mænd〕n.（對語言的）運用自如的能力；精通

27. (**D**) 誰在找家教？

(A) 一位大學畢業生。

(B) 一位住在萬芳醫院站附近的男士。

(C) 一位會講英文的人。

(D) 吳小姐。

* *look for* 尋找

28. (**B**) 哪個人不會得到這份工作？

　　(A) 不是來自美國的人。　　(B) 星期三晚上沒空的人。

　　(C) 英文流利的人。　　(D) 在萬芳醫院工作的人。

* free〔fri〕*adj.* 有空的
  fluent〔'fluənt〕*adj.*（言語）流利的

Questions 29-30

★ *每日行駛班次* ★

🚌 **車票** 🚌

↑ 單程票—十六元　　↓↑來回票—三十元

伯里到門地		門地到伯里	
駛離伯里	到達門地	駛離門地	到達伯里
早上 6:30	早上 8:30	早上 9:00	早上 11:00
早上 11:30	下午 1:30	下午 2:00	下午 4:00
早上 4:30	早上 6:30	晚上 7:00	晚上 9:00

daily〔'delɪ〕*adj.* 每日的
service〔'sɝvɪs〕*n.*（火車、公車等的）行駛；班次
one way 單程旅程（這裡指單程票）
round trip 來回旅程（這裡指來回票）　leave〔liv〕*v.* 駛離
arrive〔ə'raɪv〕*v.* 抵達　*am* 早上　*pm* 下午

29. (**C**) 如果你在早上八點半抵達門地，並且整天和一個朋友待在那裡，你若要搭巴士回家，則到伯里的最後一班巴士何時出發？

(A) 下午二點。

(B) 下午四點。

(C) 晚上七點。

(D) 晚上九點。

* spend〔spɛnd〕v. 度過　　last〔læst〕adj. 最後的

　 take〔tek〕v. 搭乘　　bus〔bʌs〕n. 公車；巴士

30. (**D**) 下列敘述何者正確？

(A) 早上從門地到伯里的班次有兩班。

(B) 伯里到門地的來回票是三十二元。

(C) 早上十一點半的巴士在下午兩點鐘抵達門地。

(D) 從伯里到門地的車程要兩個鐘頭。

* trip〔trɪp〕n. 行程

Questions 31-32

January 5
A

Dear Nora,
B

    I've been here in Waterfield for two months. Ben and I spent the Easter vacation on Ben's uncle's farm.

    Every morning his uncle drove us to a lake. We fished there. Ben could not catch any fish, but I caught four big ones on the last day. We cooked the fish on a barbecue, and had them for lunch. They tasted wonderful!

    In the afternoon we worked very hard on the farm. We wanted to help his uncle. The work on the farm was not as easy as I thought, but it was interesting. Together with the letter are some pictures we took. They are beautiful, aren't they?

Sincerely,
C

Jacky
D

元月五日
A

親愛的諾拉：
B

　　我已經待在沃德菲兩個月了。班和我在他叔叔的農場過復活節假期。

　　每天早上他叔叔都開車載我們到湖邊。我們就在那裡釣魚。在最後一天，班釣不到半隻魚，但是我釣到了四隻大魚。我們把魚烤了當午餐吃。真是好吃！

　　下午我們在農場非常努力做事。我們想幫他叔叔的忙。農場的工作並不像我之前想的那麼輕鬆，但還是蠻有趣的。這封信也附了一些我們拍的照片。照片很好看，不是嗎？

傑克　敬上
D　　C

Easter (ˈistɚ) *n.* 復活節　　vacation (veˈkeʃən) *n.* 假期
uncle (ˈʌŋkḷ) *n.* 叔叔；伯父；姑丈；姨丈；舅舅
farm (farm) *n.* 農場　　drive (draɪv) *v.* 用車送 (某人)
lake (lek) *n.* 湖　　fish (fɪʃ) *v.* 釣魚　*n.* 魚
catch (kætʃ) *v.* 捕獲　　cook (kuk) *v.* 烹調；煮
barbecue (ˈbarbɪˌkju) *n.* 烤肉用的鐵架
taste (test) *v.* 嚐起來　　***as…as~*** 像～一樣…
easy (ˈizɪ) *adj.* 容易的；輕鬆的
interesting (ˈɪntrɪstɪŋ) *adj.* 有趣的　***together with*** 連同
letter (ˈlɛtɚ) *n.* 信　　picture (ˈpɪktʃɚ) *n.* 照片 (= photo
(ˈfoto))　　take (tek) *v.* 拍攝 (照片)
sincerely (sɪnˈsɪrlɪ) *adv.* 真誠地；敬上 (信件結尾用語)

31. (**A**) 如果這封信是在元月五日寫的，信中提到的照片可能是

    (A) <u>在元旦拍的。</u>   (B) 班的叔叔拍的。

    (C) 將在元月二十五日拍攝。   (D) 將在下一次寄出。

    * mention〔'mɛnʃən〕*v.* 提到

      probably〔'prɑbəblɪ〕*adv.* 可能

      New Year's Day 元旦   send〔sɛnd〕*v.* 寄；送

32. (**D**) _____C_____ 應該填什麼？

    (A) 親愛的諾拉：   (B) 元月五日

    (C) 傑克   (D) <u>敬上</u>

    * fill〔fɪl〕*v.* 填入

Questions 33-35

Some people might say that driving a bus is a boring job. I don't think so. Every day, I can meet people I have never seen before. I enjoy talking to them. And more importantly, I know that without me, many of them could not get to work or school. Helping people in this way gives me a good feeling. Even if there is nobody on my bus, I can watch small changes along the way. That green tree has gotten taller; the man in the red house has grown more flowers in front of his house. These are the things that make me feel satisfied.

有些人也許會說開公車是個無聊的工作。我倒不這麼認為。每天我都能遇到我以前從沒見過的人。我很喜歡跟他們聊天。而且更重要的是，我知道如果沒有我的話，很多人沒辦法上班或上學。這樣幫助人讓我覺得很不錯。即使車上沒有半個人，我沿路還能觀察到一些小小的變化。那顆綠樹長得更高了；紅色屋子裡的人在他的屋前種了更多花。這些事物讓我感到很滿足。

boring (ˈborɪŋ) adj. 無聊的　　meet (mit) v. 遇見；認識
importantly (ɪmˈpɔrtn̩tlɪ) adv. 重要地
without (wɪðˈaut) prep. 沒有　　*in this way* 用這種方式
feeling (ˈfilɪŋ) n. 感覺　　*even if* 即使
change (tʃendʒ) n. v. 改變　　along (əˈlɔŋ) prep. 沿著
along the way 沿路上　　green (grin) adj. 綠的
grow (gro) v. 種植　　*in front of* 在…前面
satisfied (ˈsætɪsˌfaɪd) adj. 滿足的

33. (**A**)　作者從事什麼工作？

(A) 公車司機。　　　　　(B) 計程車司機。

(C) 警察。　　　　　　　(D) 技工。

* *What is sb.?* 某人從事什麼工作？
writer (ˈraɪtə) n. 作者
policeman (pəˈlismən) n. 警察
mechanic (məˈkænɪk) n. 技工

34. (**C**)　作者喜歡他的工作，最重要的一點是什麼？

(A) 他可以認識各式各樣的人。

(B) 他可以不必找零。

(C) 他可以幫助人們。

(D) 他可以和人們聊天。

* thing (θɪŋ) n. 事情；某一點
different (ˈdɪfrənt) adj. 不同的
kind (kaɪnd) n. 種類
change (tʃendʒ) n. 零錢；找零
keep the change 不用找零

35. (**C**)　何者正確？

　　　(A)　當公車上沒人時，作者覺得難過。

　　　(B)　作者想換工作。

　　　(C)　作者會注意到沿路上的一些小變化。

　　　(D)　作者在公車上覺得不舒服。

　　　* sad〔sæd〕*adj.* 難過的
　　　　notice〔'notɪs〕*v.* 注意到
　　　　comfortable〔'kʌmfətəbḷ〕*adj.* 舒適的

三、寫作能力測驗

第一部份：單句寫作

第 1～5 題：句子改寫

1.　I asked Tina, "Could you open the window?"
　　I asked Tina whether ＿＿＿＿＿＿＿＿＿＿＿＿＿＿＿＿.

　　　重點結構：以 whether 引導名詞子句的用法

　　　解　　答：<u>I asked Tina whether she could open the window.</u>

　　　句型分析：I asked Tina + whether + 主詞 + 動詞

　　　說　　明：Could you open the window? 是直接問句，
　　　　　　　　現在要放在 whether（是否）後面，做為 I asked
　　　　　　　　Tina 的受詞，即名詞子句（間接問句）「連接詞
　　　　　　　　+ 主詞 + 動詞」的形式，在 I asked Tina 後面接
　　　　　　　　whether you could open the window，並把問號
　　　　　　　　改成句點。

　　　* whether〔'hwɛðɚ〕*conj.* 是否

2. Sally is shorter than all the other students in her class.

Sally ＿＿＿＿＿＿＿ shortest ＿＿＿＿＿＿＿ in her class.

重點結構：比較級表達最高級的用法

解　答：<u>Sally is the shortest student in her class.</u>

句型分析：主詞＋be 動詞＋the＋形容詞最高級＋名詞

說　明：題目的意思是「莎莉比她班上的其他學生矮」，換句話說，「沙莉是她班上最矮的學生」，可以用最高級表達，在 shortest 之前須加定冠詞 the，並把 students 改為單數名詞 student。

3. Tim didn't go to school because he didn't feel well.

Tim ＿＿＿＿＿＿＿＿＿, so ＿＿＿＿＿＿＿＿＿.

重點結構：so 的用法

解　答：<u>Tim didn't feel well, so he didn't go to school.</u>

句型分析：主詞＋動詞＋so＋主詞＋動詞

說　明：連接詞 because（因為）和 so（所以）的比較：

$$\begin{cases} 結果＋because＋原因 \\ 原因＋so＋結果 \end{cases}$$

* well〔wɛl〕adj. 身體健康的

4. Jane didn't hand in her report on time.

Why ＿＿＿＿＿＿＿＿＿＿＿＿＿＿＿＿？

重點結構：wh-問句的用法

解　答：<u>Why didn't Jane hand in her report on time?</u>

句型分析：Why＋didn't＋主詞＋原形動詞？

說　明：這一題應將過去式的否定直述句改為 wh-問句，助動詞 didn't 與主詞 Jane 倒裝即可。

* *hand in* 繳交　　report〔rɪ'port〕n. 報告　　*on time* 準時

5. Our teacher made this cake.

   This cake _____ our teacher.

    重點結構：被動語態字序

      解　答：<u>This cake was made by our teacher.</u>

    句型分析：主詞＋be 動詞＋過去分詞＋by＋受詞

    説　明：被動語態的形式是「be 動詞＋過去分詞」，故動詞 made 須改為 was made。

第6～10題：句子合併

6. Kevin has a backpack.

   The backpack is black.

   Kevin _____ backpack.

    重點結構：形容詞與名詞字序

      解　答：<u>Kevin has a black backpack.</u>

    句型分析：主詞＋動詞＋形容詞＋名詞

    説　明：表達顏色的形容詞，放在要修飾的名詞之前。

    ＊ backpack〔'bæk͵pæk〕n. 背包

7. Where are they going to?

   I'd like to know.

   I'd like to know where _____.

    重點結構：間接問句做名詞子句

      解　答：<u>I'd like to know where they are going to.</u>

    句型分析：I'd like to know＋where＋主詞＋動詞

    説　明：在 wh-問句前加 I'd like to know，形成間接問句，即「疑問詞＋主詞＋動詞」的形式，因此必須把動詞 are going to 放在最後面，並把問號改成句點。

8. Little Wendy can't sleep.

She needs to hold her blanket.

Little Wendy _____ without _____.

重點結構：without 的用法

解　答：Little Wendy can't sleep without (holding) her blanket.

句型分析：主詞＋動詞＋without＋（動）名詞

說　明：without（沒有）為介系詞，後面須接名詞或動名詞，故可接 her blanket 或 holding her blanket。

* hold〔hold〕v. 抱著
  blanket〔'blæŋkɪt〕n. 毛毯

9. I have a computer.

My computer is new and expensive.

I have _____ which _____.

重點結構：由 which 引導的形容詞子句

解　答：I have a computer which is new and expensive.

句型分析：I have a computer＋which＋動詞

說　明：句意是「我有一台電腦，這台電腦既新穎又昂貴。」在合併兩句時，用 which 代替先行詞 a computer，引導形容詞子句，在子句中做主詞。

* computer〔kəm'pjutə〕n. 電腦
  expensive〔ɪk'spɛnsɪv〕adj. 昂貴的

10. My mother is here.

My father is here, too.

Both _____ and _____.

    重點結構：both A and B 的用法

    解　答：<u>Both my mother and my father are here.</u>

    句型分析：Both + 名詞 + and + 名詞 + 動詞

    説　明：題意是「我母親跟我父親兩人都在這裡。」用「both …and～」合併兩個主詞，表「…和～兩者都」。

第 11～15 題：重組

11. Peter _____.

understanding / what / has / the child / is saying / trouble

    重點結構：「have trouble + V-ing」的用法

    解　答：<u>Peter has trouble understanding what the child is saying.</u>

    句型分析：主詞 + have trouble + 動名詞

    説　明：have trouble + V-ing 表「做…有困難」，have trouble 後面省略介系詞 in，故後面加動名詞。

12. I _____.

get up / in / at / used to / the morning / five o'clock

    重點結構：「used to + 原形 V.」的用法

    解　答：<u>I used to get up at five o'clock in the morning.</u>

    句型分析：主詞 + used to + 原形動詞

    説　明：used to 表「以前」，整句的意思是說「我以前習慣早上五點鐘起床。」

13. Keep _____!

or / get / quiet / out

重點結構：or 的用法

解　答：<u>Keep quiet or get out!</u>

句型分析：原形動詞，or + 主詞 + 動詞

說　明：這題的意思是說「安靜點，不然就出去！」，連接詞 or 表「否則」。

* keep〔kip〕v 保持住…狀態　　quiet〔'kwaɪət〕adj. 安靜的
  get out 出去

14. James _____.

looking for / for / a / house / has / a while / new / been

重點結構：現在完成進行式字序

解　答：<u>James has been looking for a new house for a while.</u>

句型分析：主詞 + have/has + been + 現在分詞 + for a while

說　明：一般現在完成進行式的結構是「主詞 + have/has + 現在分詞」，而 for a while，表「（持續）一段時間」，此時間片語須置於句尾。

* **look for** 尋找　　while〔hwaɪl〕n. 一會兒；一段時間

15. Gary _____.

as long as / is not / will / raining / jog / it

　　重點結構：as long as 的用法

　　解　答：<u>Gary will jog as long as it is not raining.</u>

　　句型分析：主詞＋動詞＋as long as＋主詞＋動詞

　　說　明：as long as 表「只要」，為連接詞片語，引導副詞子
　　　　　　句，即完整的主詞加動詞，本題的意思是「蓋瑞會去
　　　　　　慢跑，只要沒有下雨的話」。

第二部份：段落寫作

題目：現在正是暑假時期，下面是你每天的活動，請根據這些圖片
　　　寫一篇約 50 字的簡短描述。

I am very busy this summer vacation. ***In the morning*** I go to swimming school. I like to play with my friends in the water. ***In the afternoon*** I go to my English class. We play games and sing English songs. ***In the evening*** I eat dinner with my parents. I tell them what I did that day. Summer vacation is a lot of fun

summer vacation 暑假
swimming school 游泳訓練班

心得筆記欄 ✏️

全民英語能力分級檢定測驗
初級測驗②

一、聽力測驗

本測驗分三部份，全為三選一之選擇題，每部份各 10 題，共 30 題，作答時間約 20 分鐘。

第一部份：看圖辨義

本部份共 10 題，試題冊上每題有一個圖片，請聽錄音機播出一個相關的問題，與 A、B、C 三個英語敘述後，選一個與所看到圖片最相符的答案，並在答案紙上相對的圓圈內塗黑作答。每題播出一遍，問題及選項均不印在試題冊上。

例：（看）

NT$80

NT$50

（聽）

Look at the picture.　How much is the hamburger?

  A.　It's eighty dollars.
  B.　It's fifty-five dollars.
  C.　It's eighteen dollars.

正確答案為 A

Question 1

Question 2

Question 3

Question 4

Question 5

Question 6

請 翻 頁 ▊⟹

Question 7

Question 8

Question 9

Question 10

請 翻 頁 ▯▯▯⇒

第二部份：問答

本部份共 10 題，每題錄音機會播出一個問句或直述句，
每題播出一次，聽後請從試題冊上 A、B、C 三個選項中，
選出一個最適合的回答或回應，並在答案紙上塗黑作答。

例：

（聽） Good morning, Kevin. How are you?

（看） A. I'm fine, thank you.
　　　 B. I'm in the living room.
　　　 C. My name is Kevin.

正確答案為 A

11. A. Yes, it's my book.
　　B. It's on the desk.
　　C. It was a very good
　　　 book.

12. A. I went bowling last
　　　 Sunday.
　　B. I play tennis with
　　　 my sister.
　　C. Sunday is my favorite
　　　 day of the week.

13. A. I will, doctor.
　　B. Here you are, nurse.
　　C. No, thank you.

14. A. I will finish it tonight.
　　B. I finished it
　　　 yesterday.
　　C. No, I don't.

15. A. Sorry. I don't have
    time now.
    B. In one hour.
    C. It's exactly 5:25.

16. A. A little, thanks
    B. No thanks, just soup
    C. Two ices, please.

17. A. Let's just have
    coffee.
    B. Around seven
    o'clock.
    C. About 15 minutes.

18. A. No, she's my cousin.
    B. Yes, he is.
    C. Yes, my sister is a
    girl.

19. A. Of course. Make
    yourself at home.
    B. Don't mention it.
    C. Who said so?

20. A. It was harder than I
    expected.
    B. It was at nine o'clock.
    C. It was in room 101.

請 翻 頁 ‖⟹

第三部份： 簡短對話

本部份共 10 題，每題錄音機會播出一段對話及一個相關的問題，每題播出兩次，聽後請從試題冊上 A、B、C 三個選項中，選出一個最適合的回答，並在答案紙上塗黑作答。

例：

（聽）(Woman)　Good afternoon, ...Mr. Davis?

(Man)　Yes.　I have an appointment with Dr. Sanders at two o'clock.　My son Tommy has a fever.

(Woman)　Oh, that's too bad.　Well, please have a seat, Mr. Davis.　Dr. Sanders will be right with you.

Question:　Where did this conversation take place?

（看）A.　In a post office.

B.　In a restaurant.

C.　In a doctor's office.

正確答案為 C

21. A. A small one.
    B. A dog.
    C. A fish.

22. A. He gave the girl a
       book report.
    B. He put the book
       down.
    C. He return the book.

23. A. Show the girl how
       to make the soup.
    B. Help the girl with
       her homework.
    C. Give the girl some
       more soup.

24. A. He is a dentist.
    B. He is a repairman.
    C. He is a cook.

25. A. An art class.
    B. A photo shop.
    C. A bookstore.

26. A. They are going to be late.
    B. They are in a traffic jam.
    C. They are going to a
       theater.

27. A. She is a lawyer.
    B. She is a homemaker.
    C. We don't know.

28. A. By plane.
    B. By train.
    C. By car.

29. A. He was too tired.
    B. The baby was crying.
    C. He has an important
       meeting today.

30. A. Give a birthday
       party for her husband.
    B. Answer the phone.
    C. Go to a party at her
       house next week.

請 翻 頁 ⇒

二、閱讀能力測驗

本測驗分三部份，全爲四選一之選擇題，共 35 題，作答時間 35 分鐘。

第一部份：詞彙和結構

本部份共 15 題，每題含一個空格。請就試題冊上 A、B、C、D 四個選項中選出最適合題意的字或詞，標示在答案紙上。

1. In Japan, people bow to each other when they meet, but in the U.S., people _____ hands to greet each other.
   A. catch
   B. clap
   C. shake
   D. touch

2. I often read _____ of new movies before I go to the movies.
   A. links
   B. dialogues
   C. reviews
   D. songs

3. This is my _____ record, and I love her beautiful voice most.
   A. favorite
   B. true
   C. active
   D. legal

4. The doctor examined Steve carefully and wrote a _____ for him.
   A. pollution
   B. prescription
   C. vacation
   D. conversation

5. John _____ foreign coins, and he has a large number of different foreign coins.
   A. connects
   B. collects
   C. continues
   D. communicates

6. Can you look at my computer? It looks like there is something wrong _____ my computer.
   A. in
   B. with
   C. to
   D. for

7. Robert : _____ are you going to get to Taichung?
   Morgan : I will go by train and I have bought the ticket.
   A. When
   B. Why
   C. Where
   D. How

請 翻 頁 ⑩⟹

8. _____ you go to the new shopping mall last weekend?
The traffic around the mall was terrible!
A. Are
B. Have
C. Did
D. Can

9. The chocolate milk in the glass _____ for you. Remember
to drink it before you go to school.
A. are
B. is
C. have
D. has

10. Listen, the baby _____. Maybe she is hungry now.
A. cries
B. is crying
C. has cried
D. cried

11. To be a good learner _____ not an easy job.
A. is
B. are
C. has
D. have

12. Who is the person _____ sent you a birthday card?
    A. which
    B. that
    C. who
    D. ×

13. The Pacific Ocean is _____ than the Atlantic Ocean.
    A. big
    B. biger
    C. bigger
    D. the biggest

14. I can't find my dictionary. Have you seen _____?
    A. them
    B. one
    C. it
    D. its

15. Jessica _____ exercise in the gym after work. That's
    why she is always full of energy.
    A. get usually
    B. usually get
    C. gets usually
    D. usually gets

請 翻 頁 ⫸

第二部份: 段落填空

本部份共 10 題,包括二個段落,每個段落各含 5 個空格。
請就試題冊上 A、B、C、D 四個選項中選出最適合題意
的字或詞,標示在答案紙上。

Questions 16-20

Many students now spend too much time ___(16)___ TV.
After they ___(17)___ school, the first thing they do is sit down
in front of the television. They don't turn off the TV until all the
programs are over. My mother does not think TV is ___(18)___
for children. She lets us ___(19)___ only one program a night. She
is ___(20)___ we would forget our homework because watching
TV is more interesting than studying.

16. A. watch
　　B. to watch
　　C. watching
　　D. to watching

17. A. come back from
　　B. think about
　　C. out of
　　D. go to

18. A. poor
　　B. bad
　　C. strong
　　D. good

19. A. watch
　　B. to watch
　　C. watching
　　D. to watching

20. A. satisfied
　　B. glad
　　C. surprised
　　D. worried

Questions 21-25

A telephone call from a friend is always a happy thing. But it is not ___(21)___ you are having dinner, taking a bath, ___(22)___ getting ready to go out for a meeting that you are already late for. A phone call may be very important to you, but it cannot be put away and ___(23)___ again like a letter. Every letter you ___(24)___ is wonderful even if it is only a short one to say hello. The person writing the letter is trying to tell you that he is thinking about you and ___(25)___ you are a special friend.

21. A. before
    B. after
    C. if
    D. why

22. A. also
    B. or
    C. be
    D. but

23. A. taken out
    B. turned on
    C. shut up
    D. turned off

24. A. write
    B. mail
    C. review
    D. get

25. A. that
    B. which
    C. who
    D. because

請 翻 頁 ◀◁⟹

第三部份： 閱讀理解

　　　　　本部份共 10 題，包括數段短文，每段短文後有 1～3 個相
　　　　　關問題，請就試題冊上 A、B、C、D 四個選項中選出最
　　　　　適合者，標示在答案紙上。

<u>Question 26</u>

DO NOT MAKE NOISE

PATIENTS RESTING

---

26. Where would you most likely see this sign?

A. In a library.

B. At school.

C. In a hospital.

D. In a classroom.

Questions 27-28

This is Tommy's schedule in February.

SUN	MON	TUE	WED	THU	FRI	SAT
English cram school 1	First day of class 2	Nina's birthday 3	4	5	6	Dinner with Bob 7
8	9	10	Dentist appointment 11	12	Basketball game 13	Movie with aunt 14
English cram school 15	16	17	18	19	20	21
22	23	24	25	26	27	Class reunion 28

27. When will Tommy see the doctor?

A. On February 3rd. B. On February 11th.

C. On February 13th. D. On February 28th.

28. What do we know from Tommy's schedule?

A. He will see his old classmates on February 28th.

B. The school starts on Sunday.

C. He will see a movie with Nina on her birthday.

D. He will have English classes on Saturday.

請 翻 頁 ▯▭⟹

Questions 29-31

Dear Dr. Problem,

My mother is on a diet. My sister is on a diet. My grandmother is on a diet. I am *NOT* on a diet, and there is nothing good to eat in my house. I like steak, pork chops, potatoes and rice. I want an ice cream or a pizza *NOW*! My mother is eating only salad and fish. My sister is eating only carrots, cucumbers, and tomatoes. My grandmother is eating only chicken and lettuce. I am STARVING! What can I do?

A Hungry Boy

Dear Hungry,

Eat at a friend's house. Eat the food you like at lunch. Learn to like salad and fish and chicken. Buy some snacks and eat them before you go home. But be careful! You don't want to be on a diet, too.

Dr. Problem

29. What is Hungry Boy's problem?

    A. He is too heavy.

    B. He is too thin.

    C. He doesn't like the food his family eats.

    D. He cannot eat fish.

30. Which food is not eaten by any of Hungry Boy's dieting
    families?

    A. Chicken.

    B. Cucumbers.

    C. Potatoes.

    D. Carrots.

31. What does Dr. Problem suggest Hungry Boy do?

    A. Go on a diet, too.

    B. Buy his mother some snacks.

    C. Stop eating the food he likes.

    D. Have meals at his friend's house.

請 翻 頁 ⟦⇒

Questions 32-33

What would happen to our education if there were no teachers and students in schools? Would it mean that children wouldn't study anymore? The answer is no.

Some teachers and students are happy to know that in the future, they will not have to go to school every day. They will see each other on their computers. When all the computers are connected, teachers will teach on the computer network. The biggest difference is that there will be no more papers to hand in because students will do all their homework on a computer.

32. What will teachers do in the future?
   A. They will teach computer classes.
   B. They will only teach students that like to study.
   C. They will teach students by computer.
   D. They will not give their students any homework.

33. Which of the following is true?
   A. Students will have much homework in computer classes.
   B. When students can take classes on the computer network, they will not have to go to school.
   C. Students will do their homework at home, but go to school to hand it in.
   D. Teachers will use the computer network to play games.

Questions 34-35

Saint Louis's Elementary School
First Language of Students

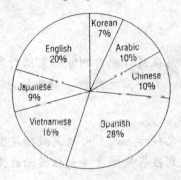

34. What percent come from families whose first language is
    not English?

    A. 20%.

    B. 10%.

    C. 80%.

    D. 28%.

35. Which of the following is **NOT** true?

    A. There are more Spanish speakers at this school than
       any other group.

    B. There are more Chinese-speaking students than
       Japanese-speaking students.

    C. 42% of the students are from Asian countries.

    D. There are as many Korean speakers as there are Arabic
       speakers.

請翻頁 ◖⟹

三、寫作能力測驗

本測驗共有兩部份，第一部份為單句寫作，第二部份為段落寫作。測驗時間為 40 分鐘。

第一部份：單句寫作

請將答案寫在寫作能力測驗答案紙對應的題號旁，如有拼字、標點、大小寫之錯誤，將予扣分。

第 1～5 題：句子改寫

請依題目之提示，將原句改寫成指定型式，並將改寫的句子完整地寫在答案紙上（包括提示之文字及標點符號）。

1. How much money does Ellen have?
   I'm not sure how much _____.

2. Would you not smoke here?
   I don't want _____.

3. Taipei is bigger than any other city in Taiwan.
   Taipei _____ biggest _____ in Taiwan.

4. I will never ride a roller coaster again!
   Never _____!

5. Rose felt sleepy, so she went to bed early.
   Rose _____ because _____.

第 6～10 題：句子合併

請依照題目指示，將兩句合併成一句，並將合併的句子完整地寫在答案紙上（包括提示之文字及標點符號）。

6. I enjoyed the movie.

   We saw it last Friday.

   I enjoyed the movie _____ last Friday.

7. Sylvia is very friendly.

   Everyone in the office likes to talk to her.

   Sylvia is so _____.

8. Heavy traffic wastes people's time.

   Heavy traffic also produces serious air pollution.

   Heavy traffic not only _____.

9. Vivian studied for three hours.

   Then, she got out to get some sunshine.

   Vivian _____ before _____.

10. I want to see the scary movie.

    My friend doesn't want to see the scary movie.

    I _____ the scary movie, _____ it.

第11~15題：重組

　　請將題目中所有提示字詞整合成一有意義的句子，並將重組的句子完整地寫在答案紙上（包括提示之文字及標點符號）。答案中必須使用所有提示字詞，且不能隨意增加字詞，否則不予計分。

11. Chris _____.
    since / interested in / has / English / he / been / child / was / a

12. Winnie _____.
    such / have / feels / strict / lucky / to / a / teacher / so

13. George _____.
    the ceiling / too / reach / short / is / to

14. The _____.
    writing / policeman / a / is / parking ticket

15. Teresa _____.
    take out / her father / forgot / the / to / for / garbage

第二部份：段落寫作

題目：今天你運氣不好，碰到一連串不如意的事，請根據圖片內容寫
　　　一篇約 50 字的簡短描述。

初級英檢模擬試題②詳解

一、聽力測驗

Look at the picture for question 1.

1. (**A**) What is not allowed in the restaurant?
   A. Smoking.
   B. He is waiting.
   C. It is cold.

   * allow〔ə'laʊ〕v. 允許　　restaurant〔'rɛstərənt〕n. 餐廳
     smoke〔smok〕v. 抽煙　　wait〔wet〕v. 等待

Look at the picture for question 2.

2. (**C**) What does the girl in the chair want?
   A. She has long hair.
   B. To dye hair.
   C. Shorter hair.

   * hair〔hɛr〕n. 頭髮　　dye〔daɪ〕v. 染

Look at the picture for question 3.

3. (**B**) What will the teacher do?
   A. She will smoke a cigarette.
   B. She will hit the students who smoke.
   C. She will sing a song.

   * cigarette〔'sɪgə‚rɛt〕n. 香煙
     hit〔hɪt〕v. 打

Look at the picture for question 4.

4. (**C**) Where are they playing volleyball?

    A. They are on the towels.

    B. There are four.

    C. At the beach.

    * volleyball ('valı,bɔl) n. 排球

      towel ('tauəl) n. 毛巾

      beach (bitʃ) n. 海灘

Look at the picture for question 5.

5. (**B**) What will she buy?

    A. New boots.

    B. A dress and shoes.

    C. A cashier.

    * boots (buts) n. pl. 靴子   dress (drɛs) n. 洋裝

      cashier (kæ'ʃɪr) n. 出納員

Look at the picture for question 6.

6. (**C**) What happened to the boy?

    A. It is bus number 110.

    B. He is jogging.

    C. He missed the bus.

    * *happen to* 發生   number ('nʌmbɚ) v. 號碼；…號

      jog (dʒɑg) v. 慢跑   miss (mɪs) v. 錯過

Look at the picture for question 7.

7. (**B**) How does he feel?

    A. He is hungry.

    B. He is tired.

    C. It is two thirty-five.

    * hungry〔'hʌŋgrɪ〕*adj.* 飢餓的

      tired〔taɪrd〕*adj.* 疲倦的

Look at the picture for question 8.

8. (**B**) What kind of test is it?

    A. It is a zero.

    B. It is a math test.

    C. It is a good test.

    * kind〔kaɪnd〕*n.* 種類   test〔tɛst〕*n.* 測驗；小考

      zero〔'zɪro〕*n.* 零分   math〔mæθ〕*n.* 數學

Look at the picture for question 9.

9. (**A**) What does she think of the coat?

    A. It is too expensive.

    B. It is too big.

    C. It can fly.

    * *think of* 認為   coat〔kot〕*n.* 外套

      expensive〔ɪk'spɛnsɪv〕*adj.* 昂貴的

      fly〔flaɪ〕*v.* 飛

Look at the picture for question 10.

10. (**C**) Where is the cat?

    A. It is sleeping.   B. It is a cat.

    C. It is on the TV.

第二部份

11. (**B**) Where is your book?

    A. Yes, it's my book.

    B It's on the desk.

    C. It was a very good book.

12. (**B**) What do you usually do on Sundays?

    A. I went bowling last Sunday.

    B. I play tennis with my sister.

    C. Sunday is my favorite day of the week.

    * usually (ˈjuʒʊəlɪ) *adv.* 通常

    on Sundays 每個星期日 (= *every Sunday*)

    go bowling 去打保齡球   *play tennis* 打網球

    favorite (ˈfevərɪt) *adj.* 最喜愛的

13. (**A**) Remember to take two pills every four hours.

    A. I will, doctor.   B. Here you are, nurse.

    C. No, thank you.

    * *remember to* + *V.* 記得要~

    take (tek) *v.* 服用 (藥物)   pill (pɪl) *n.* 藥丸

    every four hours 每隔四小時

    Here you are. 拿去吧。   nurse (nɝs) *n.* 護士

14. (**C**) Do you always finish your homework on time?

    A. I will finish it tonight.

    B. I finished it yesterday.

    C. No, I don't.

    * finish〔'fɪnɪʃ〕v. 完成

    homework〔'hom,wɜk〕n. 作業　　*on time* 準時

15. (**C**) What time is it now?

    A. Sorry. I don't have time now.

    B. In one hour.

    C. It's exactly 5:25.

    * *In one hour*. 再過一個小時。

    exactly〔ɪg'zæktlɪ〕adv. 恰好

16. (**A**) Would you like ice in your drink?

    A. A little, thanks.

    B. No thanks, just soup.

    C. Two ices, please.

    * ice〔aɪs〕n. 冰（不可數名詞）；冰淇淋（可數名詞）

    drink〔drɪŋk〕n. 飲料　　soup〔sup〕n. 湯

17. (**B**) What time do you eat breakfast?

    A. Let's just have coffee.

    B. Around seven o'clock.

    C. About 15 minutes.

    * *have coffee* 喝咖啡　　around〔ə'raʊnd〕prep. 大約

18. (**A**) Is that girl your sister?

    A. No, she's my cousin.

    B. Yes, he is.

    C. Yes, my sister is a girl.

    * cousin〔'kʌzn̩〕*n.* 堂（表）兄弟姊妹

19. (**A**) May I come in?

    A. Of course. Make yourself at home.

    B. Don't mention it.

    C. Who said so?

    * *Make yourself at home.* 不用拘束。

      Don't mention it. 不客氣。(= *You're welcome.*)

20. (**A**) How was the exam?

    A. It was harder than I expected.

    B. It was at nine o'clock.

    C. It was in room 101.

    * exam〔ɪg'zæm〕*n.* 考試

      hard〔hɑrd〕*adj.* 困難的

      expect〔ɪk'spɛkt〕*v.* 預期

第三部份

21. (**B**) W: Do you like animals?

M: Yes, especially dogs. But I don't have one.

W: Why not?

M: My house is too small.

Question: What kind of pet would the boy like most?

A. A small one.

B. A dog.

C. A fish.

* animal (ˈænəml̩) *n.* 動物
especially (əˈspɛʃəlɪ) *adv.* 尤其是
kind (kaɪnd) *n.* 種類   pet (pɛt) *n.* 寵物

22. (**C**) M: Here is the book I borrowed from you.

W: Thanks. What did you think of it?

M: It was great. I couldn't put it down.

Question: What did the boy do?

A. He gave the girl a book report.

B. He put the book down.

C. He returned the book.

* borrow (ˈbaro) *v.* 借 (入)
What do you think of it? 你認為它怎麼樣？
great (gret) *adj.* 很棒的   ***put down*** 放下
report (rɪˈport) *n.* 報告   return (rɪˈtɜn) *v.* 歸還

23. (**A**) W: This soup is delicious.

M: Thanks. It's really very easy to make.

W: Can you teach me?

M: Sure.

Question: What will the boy do?

A. Show the girl how to make the soup.

B. Help the girl with her homework.

C. Give the girl some more soup.

* delicious (dɪ'lɪʃəs) *adj.* 美味的   sure (ʃur) *adv.* 當然
  show (ʃo) *v.* 教；告訴 (某人)
  help sb. with sth. 幫助某人做某事

24. (**A**) M: What seems to be the problem?

W: Well, it hurts when I eat anything cold.

M: Hmm. Open your mouth and let me take a look.

Question: What is the man?

A. He is a dentist.

B. He is a repairman.

C. He is a cook.

* seem (sim) *v.* 似乎   problem ('prɑbləm) *n.* 問題
  hurt (hɜt) *v.* 疼痛   mouth (mauθ) *n.* 嘴巴
  let (lɛt) *v.* 讓   *take a look* 看一眼
  What is the man? 那男人從事什麼行業？ (= *What does
    the man do?*)   dentist ('dɛntɪst) *n.* 牙醫
  repairman (rɪ'pɛrmən) *n.* 修理工人
  cook (kuk) *n.* 廚師

25. (**B**) M: I'd like to have this film developed.

W: What size prints do you want?

M: Standard size, please. When will the pictures be ready?

W: It will take about one hour.

Question: Where did this conversation take place?

A. An art class.

B. A photo shop.

C. A bookstore.

* film〔fɪlm〕n. 底片

develop〔dɪ'vɛləp〕v. (底片) 沖洗；顯像

size〔saɪz〕n. 尺寸；大小

print〔prɪnt〕n. (印出的) 照片

standard〔'stændəd〕adj. 標準的

picture〔'pɪktʃə〕n. 照片 (= photo〔'foto〕)

ready〔'rɛdɪ〕adj. 準備好的　　take〔tek〕v. 花費 (時間)

conversation〔,kɑnvə'seʃən〕n. 對話

take place 發生　　art〔ɑrt〕n. 美術

photo shop 照片沖洗店

bookstore〔'buk,stor〕n. 書店

26. (**C**) M: This traffic is terrible.

W: You're right. We're barely moving.

M: I hope we won't be late for the movie.

W: Don't worry. We still have lots of time.

Question: Where are the man and the woman going?

A. They are going to be late.

B. They are in a traffic jam.

C. They are going to a theater.

* traffic ('træfɪk) *n.* 交通　　terrible ('tɛrəbl̩) *adj.* 糟糕的
  barely ('bɛrlɪ) *adv.* 幾乎不 (= *hardly*)
  move (muv) *v.* 移動　　late (let) *adj.* 遲到的
  worry ('wɝɪ) *v.* 擔心　　*lots of* 很多的 (= *a lot of*)
  a traffic jam 交通阻塞　　theater ('θiətɚ) *n.* 電影院

27. (**C**) W: What does your father do?

M: My father is a lawyer.

W: What about your mother?

M: She stays home and takes care of the family.

Question: What is the girl's mother?

A. She is a lawyer.

B. She is a homemaker.

C. We don't know.

* *What does sb. do?* 某人從事何種行業？
  lawyer ('lɔjɚ) *n.* 律師　　*What about ~?* 那~呢？
  stay (ste) *v.* 停留　　*take care of* 照顧
  homemaker ('hom,mekɚ) *n.* 家庭主婦 (= *housewife*)

28. (**B**) W: Do you know when we will arrive in Taipei?

M: This is an express, so we should be there in about 15 minutes.

W: So soon! I'm glad I decided not to drive.

Question: How are the woman and the man traveling to Taipei?

A. By plane.　　　　B. By train.

C. By car.

* arrive〔ə'raɪv〕v. 到達　　express〔ɪk'sprɛs〕n. 快車
in about 15 minutes 大約再過十五分鐘
soon〔sun〕adv. 快　　glad〔glæd〕adj. 高興的
decide〔dɪ'saɪd〕v. 決定　　drive〔draɪv〕v. 開車
travel〔'trævḷ〕v. 前進　　**travel to** 前往~
plane〔plen〕n. 飛機

29. (**B**) W: You look tired. What's wrong?

M: The baby cried all night and I didn't sleep.

W: You should take a rest now.

M: I can't. I have an important meeting at work today.

Question: Why didn't the man sleep last night?

A. He was too tired.　　B. The baby was crying.

C. He has an important meeting today.

* **What's wrong?** 怎麼了？(= **What's the matter?**)
cry〔kraɪ〕v. 哭　　**take a rest** 休息一下
important〔ɪm'pɔrtṇt〕adj. 重要的
meeting〔'mitɪŋ〕n. 會議
at work 在工作地點；在辦公室

30. (**C**) M: Who was on the phone?

W: That was our neighbor, Mrs. Li.

M: What did she want?

W: She invited us to her husband's birthday party next week.

Question: What does Mrs. Li want the man and the woman to do?

A. Give a birthday party for her husband.

B. Answer the phone.

C. Go to a party at her house next week.

* **on the phone** 電話中　neighbor ('nebɚ) n. 鄰居
invite (ɪn'vaɪt) v. 邀請　**give a party** 舉辦宴會
answer ('ænsɚ) v. 接 (電話)

二、閱讀能力測驗

第一部份：詞彙和結構

1. (**C**) In Japan, people bow to each other when they meet, but in the U.S., people shake hands to greet each other.

在日本，人們見面時彼此鞠躬，但是在美國，人們握手來打招呼。

(A) catch (kætʃ) v. 捕捉

(B) clap (klæp) v. 鼓掌

(C) **shake** (ʃek) v. 搖動　**shake hands** 握手

(D) touch (tʌtʃ) v. 碰觸

* Japan (dʒə'pæn) n. 日本　bow (baʊ) v. 鞠躬
meet (mit) v. 見面　greet (grit) v. 問候；和~打招呼

2. (**C**) I often read <u>reviews</u> of new movies before I go to the movies.

我通常在去看電影之前，會閱讀新上映的電影的<u>影評</u>。

 (A) link〔 lɪŋk 〕 *n.* 連結

 (B) dialogue〔ˈdaɪəˌlɔg 〕 *n.* 對話

 (C) ***review***〔 rɪˈvju 〕 *n.* 評論

 (D) song〔 sɔŋ 〕 *n.* 歌曲

 * ***go to the movies*** 去看電影

3. (**A**) This is my <u>favorite</u> record, and I love her beautiful voice most. 這是我<u>最喜愛的</u>唱片，我最愛她美妙的歌聲。

 (A) ***favorite***〔ˈfevərɪt 〕 *adj.* 最喜愛的

 (B) true〔 tru 〕 *adj.* 眞實的；正確的

 (C) active〔ˈæktɪv 〕 *adj.* 主動的；積極的

 (D) legal〔ˈligḷ 〕 *adj.* 合法的

 * record〔ˈrɛkəd 〕 *n.* 唱片 voice〔 vɔɪs 〕 *n.* 聲音

4. (**B**) The doctor examined Steve carefully and wrote a <u>prescription</u> for him.

醫生仔細爲史蒂夫做檢查，並且爲他開了一張<u>處方</u>。

 (A) pollution〔 pəˈluʃən 〕 *n.* 污染

 (B) ***prescription***〔 prɪˈskrɪpʃən 〕 *n.* 處方

 (C) vacation〔 veˈkeʃən 〕 *n.* 假期

 (D) conversation〔ˌkɑnvəˈseʃən 〕 *n.* 對話

 * examine〔 ɪgˈzæmɪn 〕 *v.* 檢查

 carefully〔ˈkɛrfəlɪ 〕 *adv.* 仔細地

5. (**B**) John collects foreign coins, and he has a large number
of different foreign coins.

約翰收集外國硬幣，他有非常多不同的外國硬幣。

(A) connect〔kə'nɛkt〕v. 連結
(B) *collect*〔kə'lɛkt〕v. 收集
(C) continue〔kən'tɪnju〕v. 繼續
(D) communicate〔kə'mjunə‚ket〕v. 溝通

* foreign〔'fɔrɪn〕adj. 外國的　　coin〔kɔɪn〕n. 硬幣
a large number of 許多的（= *many*）
different〔'dɪfərənt〕adj. 不同的

6. (**B**) Can you look at my computer?　It looks like there is
something wrong with my computer.

你能不能看看我的電腦？看來我的電腦好像有點問題。

wrong〔rɔŋ〕adj. 故障的；有毛病的，須接介系詞 *with*，
再接受詞。

* *look at* 看　　computer〔kəm'pjutə〕n. 電腦

7. (**D**) Robert　：How are you going to get to Taichung?
Morgan：I will go by train and I have bought the ticket.

羅伯特：你要如何去台中？
摩　根：我將坐火車去，我已經買好車票了。

從摩根的回答得知，他要搭火車去台中，詢問交通工具，
須用疑問詞 *How*，故選 (D)。而 (A) When「何時」，(B)
Why「為什麼」，(C) Where「哪裡」，皆不合句意。

* *get to* 到達　　ticket〔'tɪkɪt〕n. 車票

8. (**C**) <u>Did</u> you go to the new shopping mall last weekend?
The traffic around the mall was terrible!
你上個週末有去新開幕的購物中心嗎？購物中心附近的交通
糟透了！

> 從時間副詞 last weekend 得知，空格應填過去式助動詞
> ***Did***，選 (C)。而 (A) are 用於未來式「are going to」的
> 形式，(B) have 用於完成式「have + p.p.」的形式，故
> 用法皆不合，(D) can「能夠」，則不合句意。

> * ***shopping mall*** 購物中心 (= *mall*)
> weekend〔'wik‚εnd〕*n.* 週末　　traffic〔'træfɪk〕*n.* 交通
> around〔ə'raʊnd〕*prep.* 在～周圍
> terrible〔'tεrəbḷ〕*adj.* 糟糕的

9. (**B**) The chocolate milk in the glass <u>is</u> for you.　Remember
to drink it before you go to school.
玻璃杯裡的巧克力牛奶<u>是</u>給你的。記得去上學前把它喝掉。

> 主詞 chocolate milk 是物質名詞，為不可數名詞，故接
> 單數 be 動詞 **is**。

> * chocolate〔'tʃɔkəlɪt〕*n.* 巧克力
> glass〔glæs〕*n.* 玻璃杯

10. (**B**) Listen, the baby <u>is crying</u>.　Maybe she is hungry now.
你聽，嬰兒<u>正在哭</u>。或許她現在肚子餓了。

> listen 單獨使用時，主要功用是引起別人的注意，故常
> 與現在進行式搭配，選 (B) ***is crying***。

> * maybe〔'mebi‚'mebɪ〕*adv.* 或許

11. (**A**) To be a good learner <u>is</u> not an easy job.
要做個良好的學習者並不<u>是</u>件容易的事情。

主詞 To be a good learner 為不定詞片語，須視為單數，
故動詞要用單數 be 動詞 *is*。

* learner〔ˈlɜnɚ〕*n.* 學習者　　job〔dʒɑb〕*n.* 事情

12. (**B**) Who is the person that sent you a birthday card?
寄生日卡給你的那個人是誰？

先行詞 the person 為人，故關係代名詞用 who 或 that，
但在 Who 開頭的問句中，只能用關代 *that*，以避免重複，
造成句意混淆。

* send〔sɛnd〕*v.* 寄；送　　*birthday card* 生日卡

13. (**C**) The Pacific Ocean is <u>bigger</u> than the Atlantic Ocean.
太平洋比大西洋<u>大</u>。

從連接詞 than 可知，此為比較級的句型，big 的比較級是
bigger，故選 (C)。
* *the Pacific Ocean* 太平洋　　*the Atlantic Ocean* 大西洋

14. (**C**) I can't find my dictionary. Have you seen <u>it</u>?
我找不到我的字典。你有看到<u>它</u>嗎？

代名詞 *it* 代替先前提到的名詞 my dictionary。而 (A)
them 是複數代名詞，(B) one 代替先前提到的非特定的同
類名詞，(D) its 為所有格，用法皆不合。

* dictionary〔ˈdɪkʃən͵ɛrɪ〕*n.* 字典

15. (**D**) Jessica <u>usually gets</u> exercise in the gym after work. That's why she is always full of energy.

潔西卡下班後<u>通常</u>會去健身房運動。那就是爲什麼她總是充滿活力。

> usually (通常) 爲頻率副詞，須置於一般動詞之前，且主詞 Jessica 爲第三人稱單數，故選 (D) *usually gets*。

> * exercise (ˈɛksə‚saɪz) *n.* 運動　　gym (dʒɪm) *n.* 健身房
> *after work* 下班後　　*be full of* 充滿
> energy (ˈɛnədʒɪ) *n.* 活力

第二部份：段落填空

Questions 16-20

Many students now spend too much time <u>watching</u> TV.
                                                  16

After they <u>come back from</u> school, the first thing they do is sit
              17

down in front of the television. They don't turn off the TV until

all the programs are over. My mother does not think TV is <u>good</u>
                                                            18

for children. She lets us <u>watch</u> only one program a night. She is
                            19

<u>worried</u> we would forget our homework because watching TV is
 20

more interesting than studying.

現在有很多學生花太多時間看電視了。放學回家之後，他們第一件事就是坐在電視機前。他們會一直看，直到節目都播完了，才關掉電視。我媽媽覺得電視對兒童不好。她晚上只讓我們看一個節目。她擔心我們會忘了寫功課，因爲看電視比唸書有趣多了。

sit down 坐下來　　**in front of** 在…前面
turn off 關掉 (電器)　　until 〔 ən'tɪl 〕 *conj.* 直到
not…until~ 直到~才…　　program 〔'progræm 〕 *n.* 節目
over 〔'ovɚ 〕 *adj.* 結束的　　forget 〔 fɚ'gɛt 〕 *v.* 忘記
interesting 〔'ɪntrɪstɪŋ 〕 *adj.* 有趣的

16. (**C**) 人 + **spend** + 時間 + (**in**) + **V-ing** 某人花時間做~

17. (**A**) 依句意,學生「放學」後,故選 (A) **come back from school**。
而 (B) think about「考慮」,(D) go to school「去上學」,
則不合句意。而 (C) 須改爲 are out of,才能選。

18. (**D**) 依句意,媽媽認爲電視對小孩「沒有好處」,主要句子中已
經有 does not think,已經有否定的意思,故空格應填入 (D)
good。　be good for 對~有益

19. (**A**) let 爲使役動詞,其用法爲:「let + 受詞 + 原形動詞」,故
選 (A) **watch**。

20. (**D**) (A) satisfied 〔'sætɪs,faɪd 〕 *adj.* 滿意的
(B) glad 〔 glæd 〕 *adj.* 高興的
(C) surprised 〔 sə'praɪzd 〕 *adj.* 驚訝的
(D) **worried** 〔'wɝɪd 〕 *adj.* 擔心的

Questions 21-25

A telephone call from a friend is always a happy thing. But it is not <u>if</u> you are having dinner, taking a bath, <u>or</u> getting ready to go
　　　　21　　　　　　　　　　　　　　　　　　22
out for a meeting that you are already late for. A phone call may be very important to you, but it cannot be put away and <u>taken out</u>
　　　　　　　　　　　　　　　　　　　　　　　　　　　　　　23
again like a letter. Every letter you <u>get</u> is wonderful even if it is
　　　　　　　　　　　　　　　　　24
only a short one to say hello. The person writing the letter is trying to tell you that he is thinking about you and <u>that</u> you are
　　　　　　　　　　　　　　　　　　　　　　　　　　25
a special friend.

　　接到朋友打來的電話，總是件令人高興的事。但如果打來的時候，你正在吃晚飯、洗澡，或正準備出門趕赴你已經遲到的約會，那就不是件令人愉快的事情了。打來的電話可能對你非常重要，但你不能像看信一樣，先放著再拿出來看。接到來信讓你感覺很棒，即使只是短短的問候信件。寫信給你的人，是想讓你知道他正在想念你，而且覺得你是個特別的朋友。

> **telephone call** 電話 (= *phone call*)　　　**take a bath** 洗澡
> ready〔ˋrɛdɪ〕*adj.* 準備好的　　**go out** 外出
> meeting〔ˋmitɪŋ〕*n.* 會面；會議　　late〔let〕*adj.* 遲到的
> **put away** 收好；儲存　　letter〔ˋlɛtɚ〕*n.* 信
> wonderful〔ˋwʌndɚfəl〕*adj.* 很棒的　　**even if** 即使
> **say hello** 打招呼；問好　　**try to** *V.* 努力；設法
> **think about** 想　　special〔ˋspɛʃəl〕*adj.* 特別的

21. (**C**) 依句意，「如果」你在不方便接電話的時候有人打電話來了，那就不是件令人高興的事，故選 (C) *if*。

22. (**B**) 按照句意，列舉不方便接電話的時候，如吃晚飯、洗澡，「或」正準備出門，故用連接詞 *or*，選 (B)。

23. (**A**)　(A) *take out* 拿出來　　(B) turn on 打開（電器）
　　　　　(C) shut up 閉嘴　　　(D) turn off 關掉（電器）

24. (**D**) 依句意，「接到」信的感覺很棒，故選 (D) *get*。而 (A) write 「寫（信）」，(B) mail 「寄（信）」，(C) review「複習」，均不合句意。

25. (**A**) 依句意，and 為對等連接詞，前後要連接文法地位相同的單字、片語或子句，前面是 that 引導的名詞子句，故後面也要接 that 引導的名詞子句，都做動詞 tell 的受詞，故選 (A) *that*。

第三部份：閱讀理解

Question 26

禁 止 喧 嘩
病患休息中

make noise 製造噪音　　　patient〔'peʃənt〕*n.* 病人
rest〔rɛst〕*v.* 休息

26. (**C**) 你最有可能在哪裡看到此告示牌？
　　　　　(A) 在圖書館裡。　　　(B) 在學校內。
　　　　　(C) 在醫院裡。　　　　(D) 在教室裡。
　　　* likely〔'laɪklɪ〕*adv.* 可能　　sign〔saɪn〕*n.* 告示牌
　　　library〔'laɪˌbrɛrɪ〕*n.* 圖書館

Questions 27-28

這是湯米二月份的行程表。

星期天	星期一	星期二	星期三	星期四	星期五	星期六
英文 補習班 1	開學 第一天 2	妮娜 的生日 3	4	5	6	和鮑伯 吃晚餐 7
8	9	10	看牙醫 11	12	籃球 比賽 13	和阿姨 看電影 14
英文 補習班 15	16	17	18	19	20	21
22	23	24	25	26	27	同學會 28

schedule〔'skɛdʒul〕n. 時間表；行程表
cram school 補習班   dentist〔'dɛntɪst〕n. 牙醫
appointment〔ə'pɔɪntmənt〕n. 約會
aunt〔ænt〕n. 阿姨；姑媽   class〔klæs〕n. 全班同學
reunion〔ri'junjən〕n.（親友等的）團聚；重聚

27.（**B**）湯米何時要看醫生？

(A) 二月三日。　　　　　(B) 二月十一日。
(C) 二月十三日。　　　　(D) 二月二十八日。

28.（**A**）從湯米的行程表中，我們可以知道什麼？

(A) 他將在二月二十八日和他的老同學見面。
(B) 學校在星期天開學。
(C) 他將和妮娜在她生日那一天一起看電影。
(D) 他將在星期六上英文課。

* school〔skul〕n. 上課   start〔start〕v. 開始

Questions 29-31

Dear Dr. Problem,

My mother is on a diet. My sister is on a diet. My grandmother is on a diet. I am *NOT* on a diet, and there is nothing good to eat in my house. I like steak, pork chops, potatoes and rice. I want an ice cream or a pizza *NOW*! My mother is eating only salad and fish. My sister is eating only carrots, cucumbers, and tomatoes. My grandmother is eating only chicken and lettuce. I am STARVING! What can I do?

A Hungry Boy

親愛的問題博士：

我媽媽在減肥。我姊姊在減肥。我奶奶也在減肥。可是我沒有要減肥，家裡卻沒有任何好吃的東西了。我喜歡牛排、豬排、馬鈴薯和飯。我現在想要冰淇淋或披薩！我媽媽現在只吃沙拉和魚。我姊姊只吃胡蘿蔔、黃瓜和蕃茄。我奶奶只吃雞肉和萵苣。我快餓死了！我該怎麼辦？

餓肚子的男孩

Dear Hungry,

　　Eat at a friend's house. Eat the food you like at lunch. Learn to like salad and fish and chicken. Buy some snacks and eat them before you go home. But be careful! You don't want to be on a diet, too.

Dr. Problem

親愛的餓肚子：

　　去朋友家吃飯。午餐吃你想吃的東西。學著喜歡吃沙拉、魚跟雞肉。回家前買點零食吃。但要小心喔！你不會也想要加入減肥的行列的。

問題博士

dear〔dɪr〕adj. 親愛的　　Dr. 醫生（= doctor）
on a diet 在節食；減肥
grandmother〔'grænd,mʌðɚ〕n. 祖母　　steak〔stek〕n. 牛排
chop〔tʃap〕n.（切下的一塊）連骨的肉　　**pork chop** 豬排
potato〔pə'teto〕n. 馬鈴薯　　rice〔raɪs〕n. 米飯
ice cream 冰淇淋　　pizza〔'pitsə〕n. 披薩
salad〔'sæləd〕n. 沙拉　　carrot〔'kærət〕n. 胡蘿蔔
cucumber〔'kjukəmbɚ〕n. 黃瓜　　tomato〔tə'meto〕n. 番茄
lettuce〔'lɛtɪs〕n. 萵苣　　starve〔starv〕v. 餓死；飢餓
snack〔snæk〕n. 零食

29. (**C**) 餓肚子男孩的問題爲何？

(A) 他太胖。　　　　　　(B) 他太瘦。

(C) <u>他不喜歡家人吃的東西。</u>　(D) 他不能吃魚。

* heavy〔'hɛvɪ〕*adj.* 重的　　thin〔θɪn〕*adj.* 瘦的

30. (**C**) 餓肚子男孩的家人，減肥時不吃哪一個食物？

(A) 雞肉。　　　　　　(B) 黃瓜。

(C) <u>馬鈴薯。</u>　　　　　(D) 胡蘿蔔。

* family〔'fæmǝlɪ〕*n.* 家人

31. (**D**) 問題博士建議餓肚子男孩該怎麼辦？

(A) 也一起減肥。　　　　(B) 買一些零食給媽媽。

(C) 停止吃他喜歡的食物。　(D) <u>去朋友家吃飯。</u>

* suggest〔sǝ'dʒɛst〕*v.* 建議　　have〔hæv〕*v.* 吃
　meal〔mil〕*n.* 一餐

Questions 32-33

What would happen to our education if there were no teachers and students in schools? Would it mean that children wouldn't study anymore? The answer is no.

如果學校裡沒有老師和學生的話，我們的教育會怎樣？這表示小孩子不用再唸書了嗎？答案是否定的。

happen〔'hæpǝn〕*v.* 發生　　education〔ˌɛdʒǝ'keʃǝn〕*n.* 教育
mean〔min〕*v.* 意謂著　　**not…anymore** 不再
answer〔'ænsɚ〕*n.* 答案

Some teachers and students are happy to know that in the future, they will not have to go to school every day. They will see each other on their computers. When all the computers are connected, teachers will teach on the computer network. The biggest difference is that there will be no more papers to hand in because students will do all their homework on a computer.

有些老師和學生如果以後不用每天去學校，一定會很高興。他們可以在電腦上見面。當所有電腦都連線時，老師就可以利用網路進行教學。最大的不同就是，將不再需要交報告了，因為學生可以在電腦上做功課。

> ***in the future*** 在未來　　***go to school*** 到學校；去上學
> ***each other*** 彼此　　connect〔kə'nɛkt〕*v.* 連結
> network〔'nɛt,wɜk〕*n.*（電腦）網絡
> difference〔'dɪfrəns〕*n.* 差別　　paper〔'pepɚ〕*n.* 報告
> ***hand in*** 繳交　　homework〔'hom,wɜk〕*n.* 家庭作業；功課

32. (**C**) 老師以後將會做什麼？
    (A) 他們將教電腦課程。
    (B) 他們將只教喜歡唸書的學生。
    (C) <u>他們將利用電腦教導學生。</u>
    (D) 他們將不再給學生家庭作業。
    * by 表「藉由」。

33. (**B**) 下列敘述何者正確？
    (A) 學生電腦課的作業會很多。
    (B) <u>當學生可以用電腦網路上課時，他們將不必到學校。</u>
    (C) 學生將在家裡做作業，但要到學校交作業。
    (D) 老師將使用電腦網路玩遊戲。
    * ***take a class*** 上課

Questions 34-35

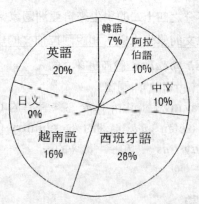

聖路易斯小學
學生的母語

elementary school 小學　　*first language* 第一語言；母語
Korean〔koˈriən〕*n.* 韓語　　Arabic〔ˈærəbɪk〕*n.* 阿拉伯語
Spanish〔ˈspænɪʃ〕*n.* 西班牙語
Vietnamese〔vɪˌɛtnɑˈmiz〕*n.* 越南語
Japanese〔ˌdʒæpəˈniz〕*n.* 日語

34. (**C**)　母語不是英文的家庭百分比有多少？

　　(A) 百分之二十。

　　(B) 百分之十。

　　(C) 百分之八十。（百分之一百減去母語為英文的百分之二十
　　　　人數，等於百分之八十）

　　(D) 百分之二十八。

　　* percent〔pəˈsɛnt〕*n.* 百分比

35. (**D**) 下列敘述何者不正確？

    (A) 這所學校說西班牙語的人數，比其他語言多。

    (B) 說中文的學生比說日文的學生多。

    (C) 有百分之四十二的學生來自亞洲國家。

    (D) 說韓文的學生人數，和說阿拉伯文的學生人數一樣多。

    * *Spanish speaker* 說西班牙文的人

    group〔grup〕*n.* 團體

    ~-speaking〔'spikɪŋ〕*adj.* 說~語言的（構成複合形容詞）

    Asian〔'eʃən〕*adj.* 亞洲的   country〔'kʌntrɪ〕*n.* 國家

    as many…as~ 和~一樣多的…

三、寫作能力測驗

第一部份：單句寫作

第 1~5 題：句子改寫

1. How much money does Ellen have?

    I'm not sure how much _____.

    重點結構：間接問句做名詞子句

      解 答：I'm not sure how much money Ellen has.

    句型分析：I'm not sure + how much money + 主詞 + 動詞

      說 明：在 wh-問句前加 I'm not sure，須改為間接問句，

             即「疑問詞 + 主詞 + 動詞」的形式，又因主詞 Ellen

             為第三人稱單數，have 須改為 has，並把問號改成

             句點。

    * sure〔ʃur〕*adj.* 確定的

2. Would you not smoke here?

   I don't want _____ _____.

   重點結構：want 的用法

   解　答：<u>I don't want you to smoke here.</u>

   句型分析：主詞＋want＋受詞＋to V.

   說　明：Would you not smoke here?「你可不可以不要在
   這裡抽煙？」為婉轉的請求，實際上就是希望對方个
   要抽煙，用 want（想要）改寫，接受詞後，須接个
   定詞。

3. Taipei is bigger than any other city in Taiwan.

   Taipei _____ biggest _____ in Taiwan.

   重點結構：比較級表達最高級的用法

   解　答：<u>Taipei is the biggest city in Taiwan.</u>

   句型分析：主詞＋be 動詞＋the＋形容詞最高級＋名詞

   說　明：題目的意思是「台北比台灣其他任何的城市都大」，
   換句話說，「台北是台灣最大的城市。」可以用最高
   級表達，在 biggest 之前須加定冠詞 the，並接單數
   名詞 city。

4. I will never ride a roller coaster again!

   Never _____.

   重點結構：Never 置於句首的用法

   解　答：<u>Never will I ride a roller coaster again!</u>

   句型分析：Never＋助動詞＋主詞＋原形動詞

   說　明：never（絕不）為否定副詞，置於句首為加強語氣
   的用法，其後的主詞與動詞須倒裝。

   * ride〔raɪd〕v. 乘坐　　*roller coaster* 雲霄飛車

5. Rose felt sleepy, so she went to bed early.

Rose _____ because_____.

重點結構：because 的用法

解　答：<u>Rose went to bed early because she felt sleepy.</u>

句型分析：主詞 + 動詞 + because + 主詞 + 動詞

説　明：連接詞 so（所以）和 because（因為）的比較：

$$\begin{cases} 原因 + so + 結果 \\ 結果 + because + 原因 \end{cases}$$

* sleepy〔'slipɪ〕*adj.* 想睡的

第 6～10 題：句子合併

6. I enjoyed the movie.

We saw it last Friday.

I enjoyed the movie _____ last Friday.

重點結構：形容詞子句的用法

解　答：<u>I enjoyed the movie which we saw last Friday.</u>

　　　或 <u>I enjoyed the movie that we saw last Friday.</u>

　　　或 <u>I enjoyed the movie we saw last Friday.</u>

句型分析：I enjoyed the movie +（關係代名詞）+ 主詞 + 動詞

説　明：句意是「我喜歡上星期五看的那一部電影」，在合併兩句時，可用 which 或 that 代替先行詞 the movie，又因關係代名詞在引導的形容詞子句中，做動詞 saw 的受詞，故可省略不寫。

7. Sylvia is very friendly.

Everyone in the office likes to talk to her.

Sylvia is so _____.

重點結構：「so + 形容詞 + that 子句」的用法

解　答：<u>Sylvia is so friendly that everyone in the office likes to talk to her.</u>

句型分析：主詞 + be 動詞 + so + 形容詞 + that + 主詞 + 動詞

説　明：這題的意思是說「席薇亞人很友善，所以辦公室裡的每個人都喜歡和她說話」，合併兩句時，用「so…that～」，表「如此…以致於～」。

* friendly 〔'frɛndlɪ 〕 adj. 友善的　　office 〔'ɔfɪs 〕 n. 辦公室

8. Heavy traffic wastes people's time.

Heavy traffic also produces serious air pollution.

Heavy traffic not only _____.

重點結構：「not only…but (also)～」的用法

解　答：<u>Heavy traffic not only wastes people's time but (also) produces serious air pollution.</u>

句型分析：主詞 + not only + 動詞 + but (also) + 動詞

説　明：這題的意思是說「交通擁擠，不僅浪費人們的時間，而且也製造嚴重的空氣污染」，合併兩句時，用「not only…but (also)～」表「不僅…，而且～」。

* heavy 〔'hɛvɪ 〕 adj. 大量的；擁擠的　　waste 〔 west 〕 v. 浪費
produce 〔 prə'djus 〕 v. 製造　　serious 〔'sɪrɪəs 〕 adj. 嚴重的
air 〔 ɛr 〕 n. 空氣　　pollution 〔 pə'luʃən 〕 n. 污染

9. Vivian studied for three hours.

   Then, she got out to get some sunshine.

   Vivian _____ before _____.

   重點結構：before 的用法

   解　答：<u>Vivian studied for three hours before she got</u>
   　　　　<u>out to get some sunshine.</u>

   　　　　或 <u>Vivian studied for three hours before getting</u>
   　　　　<u>out to get some sunshine.</u>

   句型分析：主詞 + 動詞 + before + 主詞 + 動詞

   　　　　或 主詞 + 動詞 + before + 動名詞

   説　明：then「然後」表示薇薇安先念三個小時的書，再外
   　　　　出曬太陽，現在用 before「在～之前」來表示事情
   　　　　的先後順序。而 before 有兩種詞性，若作為連接
   　　　　詞，引導副詞子句時，須接完整的主詞與動詞，即
   　　　　before she got out to get some sunshine；若作為
   　　　　介系詞，後面須接名詞或動名詞，即 before getting
   　　　　out to get some sunshine。

   * **_get out_** 外出　　　sunshine (ˈsʌnˌʃaɪn) n. 陽光

10. I want to see the scary movie.

    My friend doesn't want to see the scary movie.

    I _____ the scary movie, _____ it.

    重點結構：but 的用法

    解　答：<u>I want to see the scary movie, but my friend</u>
    　　　　<u>doesn't want to see it.</u>

    句型分析：主詞 + 動詞 + but + 主詞 + 動詞

    説　明：but 是對等連接詞，表示語氣上的轉折。

    * **_scary movie_** 恐怖片 (= _horror movie_)

第 11～15 題：重組

11. Chris _____.

since / interested in / has / English / he / been / child / was / a

重點結構：since 的用法

解　答：<u>Chris has been interested in English since he was a child.</u>

句型分析：主詞 + 動詞 + since + 主詞 + 動詞

說　明：連接詞 since 引導的副詞子句中，動詞時態用過去式，主要子句中的動詞時態則須用現在完成式，表示「從過去繼續到現在的狀態」。

* **be interested in**　對～有興趣　　since〔sɪns〕conj. 自從

12. Winnie _____.

such / have / feels / strict / lucky / to / a / teacher / so

重點結構：so 與 such 的用法

解　答：<u>Winnie feels so lucky to have such a strict teacher.</u>

句型分析：主詞 + 動詞 + so + 形容詞 + to have + such + 名詞

說　明：so 和 such 都作「如此」解，但 so 是副詞，修飾形容詞 lucky，such 則是形容詞，修飾名詞片語 a strict teacher。

* lucky〔'lʌkɪ〕adj. 幸運的　　strict〔strɪkt〕adj. 嚴格的

13. George _____.
    the ceiling / too / reach / short / is / to

    重點結構：「too…to V.」的用法

    解　答：George is too short to reach the ceiling.

    句型分析：主詞＋be 動詞＋too＋形容詞＋to V.

    説　明：這題的意思是說「喬治太矮了，用手碰不到天花
    　　　　板」，用 too…to V. 合併，表「太…以致於不～」。

    ＊ reach〔ritʃ〕v. 用手碰到　　ceiling〔'silɪŋ〕n. 天花板

14. The _____.
    writing / policeman / a / is / parking ticket

    重點結構：現在進行式字序

    解　答：The policeman is writing a parking ticket.

    句型分析：主詞＋be 動詞＋現在分詞

    説　明：這題的意思是說「警察正在開違規停車的罰單」，
    　　　　is writing 為現在進行式，即「be 動詞＋現在分詞」
    　　　　的形式。

    ＊ policeman〔pə'lismən〕n. 警察
    parking ticket 違規停車的罰單

15. Teresa _____.
    take out / her father / forgot / the / to / for / garbage

    重點結構：forget 的用法

    解　答：Teresa forgot to take out the garbage for her
    　　　　father.

句型分析：主詞 + forget + to V.

　說　明：「忘記去做某件事」用 forget + to V. 來表示，此題
　　　　　　須在 forgot（forget 的過去式）後面接不定詞。

* **take out** 拿出去　　garbage〔'gɑrbɪdʒ〕*n.* 垃圾

第二部份：段落寫作

題目；今天你運氣不好，碰到一連串不如意的事，請根據圖片內容寫
　　　一篇約 50 字的簡短描述。

I had a bad day today. I woke up at nine o'clock. I was
late for school and my teacher was angry. *Then* I dropped my
glasses. They broke. I took a bus home. *But* I left my wallet
on the bus. When I got home, I could not open the door
because I did not have my key. *What a terrible day!*

　　have a bad day 那天運氣不好　　*wake up* 醒來
　　angry〔'æŋgrɪ〕*adj.* 生氣的　　drop〔drɑp〕*v.* 掉落
　　glasses〔'glæsɪz〕*n. pl.* 眼鏡　　break〔brek〕*v.* 破碎
　　leave〔liv〕*v.* 遺留　　wallet〔'wɑlɪt〕*n.* 錢包
　　key〔ki〕*n.* 鑰匙

全民英語能力分級檢定測驗

初級測驗③

一、聽力測驗

　　本測驗分三部份，全為三選一之選擇題，每部份各 10 題，共 30 題，作答時間約 20 分鐘。

第一部份：看圖辨義

　　　　本部份共 10 題，試題冊上每題有一個圖片，請聽錄音機播出一個相關的問題，與 A、B、C 三個英語敘述後，選一個與所看到圖片最相符的答案，並在答案紙上相對的圓圈內塗黑作答。每題播出一遍，問題及選項均不印在試題冊上。

例：（看）　　　　　　　　　　　（聽）

NT$80　　NT$50

Look at the picture.　How much is the hamburger?

　　A.　It's eighty dollars.
　　B.　It's fifty-five dollars.
　　C.　It's eighteen dollars.

正確答案為 A

Question 1

Question 2

Question 3

Question 4

Question 5

Question 6

請 翻 頁 ⫸

Question 7

Question 8

Question 9

Question 10

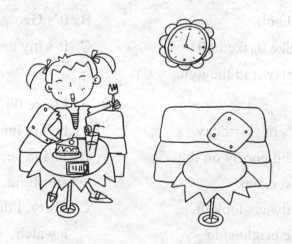

請 翻 頁 ⟹

第二部份：問答

本部份共 10 題，每題錄音機會播出一個問句或直述句，
每題播出一次，聽後請從試題冊上 A、B、C 三個選項中，
選出一個最適合的回答或回應，並在答案紙上塗黑作答。

例：

(聽) Good morning, Kevin. How are you?

(看) A. I'm fine, thank you.
    B. I'm in the living room.
    C. My name is Kevin.

正確答案爲 A

11. A. I play sports after school.
    B. I like basketball.
    C. I play it in the gym.

12. A. It's my birthday.
    B. I did poorly on the last exam.
    C. I always look on the bright side.

13. A. Pleased to meet you.
    B. It's George Brown.
    C. It's my name.

14. A. I have three hours before lunch.
    B. I have very little free time.
    C. Sorry, I don't have a watch.

15. A. They're size six.

B. There are two.

C. They're NT$1500.

16. A. Because it's a holiday

B. It's open until ten o'clock today.

C. It's close to the bank.

17. A. What's your telephone number?

B. It's for you.

C. It's your call.

18. A. I'm late for class.

B. To the library.

C. Yes, I like it very much.

19. A. For one week.

B. To Canada.

C. Yes, I'd like to.

20. A. I am not Professor Jones.

B. I'll do it as soon as I can.

C. Thank you. You shouldn't have.

請 翻 頁 ⟹

第三部份：簡短對話

　　　　本部份共 10 題，每題錄音機會播出一段對話及一個相關的問題，每題播出兩次，聽後請從試題冊上 A、B、C 三個選項中，選出一個最適合的回答，並在答案紙上塗黑作答。

　　　例：

　　　（聽）(Woman)　Good afternoon, ...Mr. Davis?

　　　　　　(Man)　　Yes.　I have an appointment with Dr. Sanders at two o'clock.　My son Tommy has a fever.

　　　　　　(Woman)　Oh, that's too bad.　Well, please have a seat, Mr. Davis.　Dr. Sanders will be right with you.

　　　　　　Question:　Where did this conversation take place?

　　　（看）A.　In a post office.

　　　　　　B.　In a restaurant.

　　　　　　C.　In a doctor's office.

　　　　正確答案爲 C

21. A. In summer.
    B. In November.
    C. Next summer.

22. A. She will send it by
       airmail.
    B. She will send it the
       fastest way.
    C. She will send it by
       surface mail.

23. A. The woman does not
       like cheese at all.
    B. The man likes
       cheese very much.
    C. The pizza will have
       some cheese on it.

24. A. Winter.
    B. Summer.
    C. Swimming.

25. A. Jane's father.
    B. Jane's friend.
    C. Jane's teacher.

26. A. He lives in a palace.
    B. He lives in a big
       building.
    C. He lives on the second
       floor.

27. A. 7:00 a.m.
    B. 2:00 p.m.
    C. 6:00 p.m.

28. A. He is a cashier.
    B. He is a patient.
    C. He is a customer.

29. A. He could not buy a
       ticket.
    B. The tickets were too
       expensive.
    C. He sold his ticket.

30. A. Take the rest of the
       medicine.
    B. Take the cold
       seriously.
    C. Take a rest.

請 翻 頁 ⟹

二、閱讀能力測驗

本測驗分三部份，全為四選一之選擇題，共 35 題，作答時間 35 分鐘。

第一部份：詞彙和結構

本部份共 15 題，每題含一個空格。請就試題冊上 A、B、C、D 四個選項中選出最適合題意的字或詞，標示在答案紙上。

1. Do some _____ exercise first, or you will hurt yourself.
   A. strict
   B. natural
   C. gentle
   D. real

2. He _____ to my question with patience. I'm satisfied with his explanation.
   A. replied
   B. answered
   C. remembered
   D. forgot

3. As soon as Carrie woke _____, she jumped out of bed.
   A. off
   B. out
   C. on
   D. up

4. Although my grandmother is 95 years old, she is still very
   _____.
   A. right
   B. healthy
   C. sick
   D. weak

5. Don't bother asking her for help. It would be a _____
   of time.
   A. waste
   B. moment
   C. space
   D. hurry

6. Helen's hair is _____ than her sister's.
   A. long
   B. much longer
   C. too longer
   D. very longer

7. Do you mind _____ I open the window?
   A. after
   B. if
   C. because
   D. although

請 翻 頁 ▮▭⇨

8. Linda and I are watching _____ favorite TV program.
   A. our
   B. ours
   C. we
   D. hers

9. Would you turn _____ the radio? I'd like to know the news about the typhoon.
   A. off
   B. up
   C. in
   D. down

10. I was busy doing my homework when the phone rang. So I stopped _____ the telephone.
    A. answering
    B. to answer
    C. answered
    D. answer

11. Without your help, I _____ have finished my report last night.
    A. shouldn't
    B. couldn't
    C. won't
    D. can't

12. I can't believe that George is doing the dishes. He _____ does any housework.

A. always

B. usually

C. hardly

D. finally

13. Andy : Does Patty go to school early?

Danny : No, she _____ late for school.

A. is often

B. often is

C. goes often

D. often goes

14. Peter and Edward are good friends. They share sorrow and joy with _____ all the time.

A. both

B. another

C. the other

D. each other

15. The waitress _____ breakfast at the restaurant every morning, but she didn't work today.

A. is serving

B. serves

C. served

D. has served

請 翻 頁 ⟹

第二部份：段落填空
　　　　　　本部份共10題，包括二個段落，每個段落各含5個空格。
　　　　　　請就試題冊上 A、B、C、D 四個選項中選出最適合題意
　　　　　　的字或詞，標示在答案紙上。

Questions 16-20

　　This summer I went to New York and stayed with an American family ___(16)___ two weeks. All the members of the family were nice ___(17)___ me. During the stay, I noticed several interesting things about their family life. For example, in my host family, the father often made dinner for us. He said, " If I helped my wife ___(18)___ cooking, we can have more time to ___(19)___ together." The trip gave me an opportunity to see the ___(20)___ between the Chinese and American's ways of life.

16. A. with
　　B. for
　　C. in
　　D. by

17. A. with
　　B. for
　　C. to
　　D. in

18. A. with
　　B. for
　　C. by
　　D. in

19. A. spend
　　B. waste
　　C. work
　　D. practice

20. A. changes
　　B. problems
　　C. languages
　　D. differences

Questions 21-25

We often see people ___(21)___ with their dogs. It is still true that a dog is the most useful ___(22)___ in the world, but the reason has changed. ___(23)___ the past, dogs were needed to watch doors. But now the reason people keep dogs in their houses is that they feel lonely in the city. For a child, a dog is his or her best friend when he or she has no friends ___(24)___. For old people, a dog is also a child when their own children have ___(25)___ and left. People keep dogs as friends, even like members of the family.

21. A. walking
    B. to walk
    C. and walk
    D. walked

22. A. machine
    B. student
    C. room
    D. animal

23. A. In
    B. On
    C. For
    D. With

24. A. to play
    B. to play with
    C. playing
    D. playing with

25. A. shut up
    B. got up
    C. stood up
    D. grown up

請 翻 頁 ⅢⲤ⟹

第三部份： 閱讀理解

本部份共 10 題，包括數段短文，每段短文後有 1～3 個相關問題，請就試題冊上 A、B、C、D 四個選項中選出最適合者，標示在答案紙上。

Question 26

PLEASE WAIT
BEHIND RED LINE

26. What does this sign mean?
    A. Wait in line.
    B. The line is busy.
    C. Stand in back of the line.
    D. Hold the line.

Questions 27-28

Renee Lin

No. 11, Lane 200 Tunghua St.

Daan Chiu, Taipei, Taiwan 106

R.O.C.

Mr. Scott Brown

3200 Las Vegas Blvd.

Las Vegas, NV 89109

AIR MAIL   U.S.A.

27. Who wrote the letter?

A. Renec.

B. Daan Chiu.

C. Tunghua St.

D. Scott.

28. Which city is the letter going to be sent to?

A. Taipei.

B. Taiwan.

C. Las Vegas.

D. U.S.A.

請 翻 頁 ⫸

Questions 29-30

ARE YOU READY?

Can you not wait to show others how great you are? Do you have a wonderful singing voice? Can you play any musical instrument well? Or do you have any special talents? Most important of all, do you like to show off in the MRT stations? Taipei Rapid Transit Corporation is looking for street performers. Come to the <u>tryouts</u> and show us how great you are!

Date : Sunday, September 15
Time : 10:00 a.m.
Place : the theater of Taipei Main Station

29. What does the Taipei Rapid Transit Corporation want people to do?
    A. Ride the MRT more often.
    B. Show off whenever they ride the MRT.
    C. Take singing lessons in the MRT.
    D. Perform in the MRT stations.

30. What word is closest in meaning to "tryout"?
    A. Sports practice.
    B. Class trip.
    C. Driving lesson.
    D. Test performance.

請 翻 頁 ⫸

Questions 31-33

Last week I went to visit my friend Emily in the hospital. She had her appendix（盲腸）taken out. She had to be hospitalized for 10 days. The doctor told her that she wouldn't be allowed to do any sports for a while. You can imagine that Emily felt very unhappy. Some of us shared the cost of a big stuffed teddy bear. We bought it for her to cheer her up. When she saw it, she started to laugh. Then she shouted, "Ouch! Ouch! Ow!" Poor Emily, I asked her if she was in pain. She answered, "Only when I laugh, Barbara. Only when I laugh."

31. From the article, what do we know about Emily?

    A. She hopes to become a doctor in the future.

    B. She did not like the teddy bear at all.

    C. She likes to play sports.

    D. She often spends time in the hospital.

32. Why did Emily go to the hospital?

    A. She worked in the hospital.

    B. She had to have an operation.

    C. She wanted to visit a sick friend.

    D. She did not want to go to school.

33. When might Emily be able to do sports again?

    A. As soon as she has her appendix taken out.

    B. In a few weeks.

    C. When she joins the hospital team.

    D. In nine days.

請 翻 頁 ◖▯⟹

Questions 34-35

5-Day Weather Forecast

Today	Tomorrow	Friday	Saturday	Sunday
Mostly Cloudy	Cloudy	Cloudy	Mostly Cloudy	Cloudy
High: 32 Low: 25	High: 35 Low: 27	High: 33 Low: 25	High: 35 Low: 25	High: 29 Low: 23

34. What is the weather like this week?

    A. Rainy.

    B. Cloudy.

    C. Sunny.

    D. Snowy.

35. Which of the following is true?

    A. Saturday's nighttime temperature will be the highest of the week.

    B. Sunday will be the warmest day of the week.

    C. Temperatures will go up tomorrow.

    D. Saturday will be the cloudiest day of the week.

三、寫作能力測驗

本測驗共有兩部份，第一部份為單句寫作，第二部份為段落寫作。測驗時間為 40 分鐘。

第一部份： 單句寫作

請將答案寫在寫作能力測驗答案紙對應的題號旁，如有拼字、標點、大小寫之錯誤，將予扣分。

第 1～5 題： 句子改寫

請依題目之提示，將原句改寫成指定型式，並將改寫的句子完整地寫在答案紙上（包括提示之文字及標點符號）。

1. I asked Amy, "Could you pass me some napkins?"

   I asked Amy if _____ pass me some napkins.

2. Helen seldom rides a bike home.

   _____ last month.

3. Lisa and her cousin played table tennis.

   When _____?

4. John : Did you go to the library to return my books?

   Nick : Oh, I forgot.

   Nick forgot _____ to return John's books.

5. To go traveling in Africa is my dream.

   It's _____.

請翻頁 ▷

第 6～10 題：句子合併

　　　　　　請依照題目指示，將兩句合併成一句，並將合併的句子
　　　　　　完整地寫在答案紙上（包括提示之文字及標點符號）。

6. Laura asked Linda something.
   The computer didn't work.

   Laura asked Linda why _____.

7. You can play video games.
   You finish your homework.

   You _____ as long as _____.

8. Patricia takes a shower.
   Then, she has dinner.

   Patricia _____ after _____.

9. Gail cleans the classroom.
   David helps her.

   David helps Gail _____.

10. I will go to the supermarket tomorrow.
    I'll mail the letter for you.

    I'll mail the letter for you when _____ tomorrow.

第 11～15 題：重組

　　　　請將題目中所有提示字詞整合成一有意義的句子，並
　　　　將重組的句子完整地寫在答案紙上（包括提示之文字
　　　　及標點符號）。答案中必須使用所有提示字詞，且不
　　　　能隨意增加字詞，否則不予計分。

11. How many _____?
    does / have / grandchildren / Vincent

12. My _____.
    goes / work / MRT / usually / by / to / father

13. Swimming _____.
    one / is / favorite / sports / my / of

14. Mr. Kelly _____.
    worked / has / for / in / years / elementary school
    / the / three

15. This _____.
    most / have / building / I / is / beautiful / the / ever / seen

請翻頁 ◀◁▭⇨

第二部份：段落寫作

題目：昨天媽媽過生日，你和弟弟一起去買禮物，最後挑了一支手錶
　　　送給媽媽，請根據圖片內容寫一篇約 50 字的簡短描述。

初級英檢模擬試題③詳解

一、聽力測驗

第一部份

Look at the picture for question 1.

1.(**B**) What time is it?
    A. It is a birthday party.   B. It is nighttime.
    C. It is a sunny day.

    * nighttime ('naɪt,taɪm) *n.* 夜間
    sunny ('sʌnɪ) *adj.* 晴朗的

Look at the picture for question 2.

2.(**C**) What did the dog do?
    A. The dog was eating.   B. He is angry.
    C. It stole some food.

    * angry ('æŋgrɪ) *adj.* 生氣的
    steal (stil) *v.* 偷 (三態變化爲 : steal-stole-stolen)

Look at the picture for question 3.

3.(**C**) Where are they sitting?
    A. They are looking at the stars.
    B. It is night.
    C. They are on a bench.

    * *look at* 看   star (star) *n.* 星星
    bench (bɛntʃ) *n.* 長椅

Look at the picture for question 4.

4. (**B**) What is in the refrigerator?
   A. It is in the kitchen.
   B. There is little food.
   C. She wants to cook.

   * refrigerator〔rɪˈfrɪdʒəˏretə〕*n.* 冰箱
     cook〔kʊk〕*v.* 煮飯；做菜

Look at the picture for question 5.

5. (**A**) What does the man want?
   A. He wants the boy to help him.
   B. He wants to wash the boy.
   C. He wants to drive the car.

Look at the picture for question 6.

6. (**C**) Why is he angry?
   A. The door is closed.
   B. The door is open.
   C. The music is too loud.

   * music〔ˈmjuzɪk〕*n.* 音樂   loud〔laʊd〕*adj.* 大聲的

Look at the picture for question 7.

7. (**A**) What is on the table?
   A. Some chicken.   B. A dog.
   C. A boy.

   * chicken〔ˈtʃɪkən〕*n.* 雞肉

Look at the picture for question 8.

8. (**C**) When will she see her boyfriend?

    A. In six hours.

    B. In her dreams.

    C. At six o'clock.

    * boyfriend (ˈbɔɪ͵frɛnd) *n.* 男朋友

    In six hours. 再過六個小時。   dream (drim) *n.* 夢

Look at the picture for question 9.

9. (**B**) Who won third place?

    A. The boy.

    B. The girl with pigtails.

    C. The girl with short, curly hair.

    * win (wɪn) *v.* 贏得 (三態變化為：win-won-won)

    place (ples) *n.* (比賽的) 名次   *third place* 第三名

    pigtail (ˈpɪg͵tel) *n.* 辮子   curly (ˈkɝlɪ) *adj.* 捲髮的

Look at the picture for question 10.

10. (**B**) What time is it?

    A. She is in a coffee shop.

    B. It is four o'clock.

    C. She is eating cake.

    * *coffee shop* 咖啡廳   cake (kek) *n.* 蛋糕

第二部份

11. (**B**) What's your favorite sport?

    A. I play sports after school.

    B. I like basketball.

    C. I play it in the gym.

    * favorite〔'fevərɪt〕*adj.* 最喜愛的   sport〔sport〕*n.* 運動

    after school 放學後   basketball〔'bæskɪt,bɔl〕*n.* 籃球

    gym〔dʒɪm〕*n.* 體育館

12. (**B**) You look upset.

    A. It's my birthday.

    B. I did poorly on the last exam.

    C. I always look on the bright side.

    * upset〔ʌp'sɛt〕*adj.* 不高興的

    do poorly 考不好（↔ *do well* ）

    last〔læst〕*adj.* 上次的   bright〔braɪt〕*adj.* 光明的

    side〔saɪd〕*n.* (事物的) 方面

    look on the bright side 看事物的光明面；往好的方面想

13. (**B**) Please give me your name.

    A. Pleased to meet you.

    B. It's George Brown.

    C. It's my name.

    * give〔gɪv〕*v.* 提供；告訴

    Pleased to meet you. 很高興認識你。

    (= *Nice to meet you.* = *Glad to meet you.*)

14. (**C**) What time do you have?

    A. I have three hours before lunch.

    B. I have very little free time.

    C. Sorry, I don't have a watch.

    * ***What time do you have?*** 現在幾點幾分？

      (= *What time is it?* = *Do you have the time?*)

    free time 空閒時間

15. (**C**) How much are these shoes?

    A. They're size six.   B. There are two.

    C. They're NT$1500.

    * size〔saɪz〕*n.* 尺寸

16. (**B**) What time does the store close?

    A. Because it's a holiday.

    B. It's open until ten o'clock today.

    C. It's close to the bank.

    * close〔kloz〕*v.* (商店) 打烊　〔klos〕*adj.* 接近的 < *to* >

    holiday〔'hɑlə,de〕*n.* 假日　　until〔ən'tɪl〕*prep.* 直到

    bank〔bæŋk〕*n.* 銀行

17. (**A**) Please give me a call.

    A. What's your telephone number?

    B. It's for you.

    C. It's your call.

    * ***give sb. a call*** 打電話給某人　　number〔'nʌmbɚ〕*n.* 號碼

    It's for you. 你的電話。　　***It's your call.*** 由你來決定。

18. (**A**) Why are you running?
    A. I'm late for class.
    B. To the library.
    C. Yes, I like it very much.

    * late〔let〕*adj.* 遲到的
      library〔ˈlaɪˌbrɛrɪ〕*n.* 圖書館

19. (**B**) Where are you going for your vacation?
    A. For one week.
    B. To Canada.
    C. Yes, I'd like to.

    * vacation〔veˈkeʃən〕*n.* 假期
      Canada〔ˈkænədə〕*n.* 加拿大

20. (**B**) Please give this to Professor Jones.
    A. I am not Professor Jones.
    B. I'll do it as soon as I can.
    C. Thank you. You shouldn't have.

    * professor〔prəˈfɛsə〕*n.* 教授
      as soon as one can 儘快 (= *as soon as possible*)
      You shouldn't have. 你不用這麼做的；你太客氣了。

第三部份

21. (**B**) W: When are you going to New York?

M: I was hoping to go in July, but it looks like I'll have to wait until November.

W: That's too bad. The summer would be a nice time to be there.

Question: When is the man going to New York?

A. In summer.

B. In November.

C. Next summer.

* hope〔hop〕v. 希望　*New York* 紐約
That's too bad. 眞可惜。

22. (**C**) W: How much will it cost to send this package by airmail?

M: That would be 700 NT dollars.

W: How about by surface mail?

M: It would cost 83 dollars.

W: I'll send it the cheaper way.

Question: How will the woman send the package?

A. She will send it by airmail.

B. She will send it the fastest way.

C. She will send it by surface mail.

* send〔sɛnd〕v. 寄　package〔'pækɪdʒ〕n. 包裹
airmail〔'ɛr,mel〕n. 航空郵件　*by airmail* 以航空郵件
surface〔'sɝfɪs〕adj. 陸路的；水路的
surface mail 普通郵件　way〔we〕n. 方式

23. (**C**) M: What would you like on your pizza?

W: Some ham, corn, and pineapple.

M: Would you like extra cheese?

W: No, thanks. Just the regular amount.

Question: Which of the following is true?

A. The woman does not like cheese at all.

B. The man likes cheese very much.

C. The pizza will have some cheese on it.

* pizza〔'pitsə〕 n. 披薩　　ham〔hæm〕 n. 火腿
 corn〔kɔrn〕 n. 玉米　　pineapple〔'paɪn͵æpḷ〕 n. 鳳梨
 extra〔'ɛkstrə〕 adj. 額外的
 cheese〔tʃiz〕 n. 乳酪；起司
 regular〔'rɛgjələ〕 adj. 一般的
 amount〔ə'maʊnt〕 n. 數量
 following〔'faləwɪŋ〕 adj. 以下的
 true〔tru〕 adj. 真實的；正確的　　*not…at all* 一點也不

24. (**B**) M: It's my favorite time of year because we have a
 long vacation.

W: I don't like it. It's too hot.

M: I don't mind the heat because I like to swim.

Question: What season are they talking about?

A. Winter.　　　　B. Summer.

C. Swimming.

* mind〔maɪnd〕 v. 介意　　heat〔hit〕 n. 熱
 swim〔swɪm〕 v. 游泳　　season〔'sizn̩〕 n. 季節
 talk about 談論

25. (**C**) M : Jane, what will you do during the summer holiday?

W : My friends and I are going to travel around the island.

M : That sounds like fun, but don't forget your homework.

W : Do I really have to write the report this summer?

M : Yes. You must hand it in on the first day of class or I will have to give you a zero.

Question : Who is the man?

A. Jane's father.　　　B. Jane's friend.

C. Jane's teacher.

* during ('djʊrɪŋ) *prep.* 在…期間　　　travel ('trævl̩) *v.* 旅行
around (ə'raʊnd) *prep.* 在…四處
island ('aɪlənd) *n.* 島嶼
travel around the island 環島旅行　　　fun (fʌn) *n.* 樂趣
forget (fə'gɛt) *v.* 忘記　　　report (rɪ'port) *n.* 報告
hand in 繳交　　　zero ('zɪro) *n.* 零分

26. (**B**) W : Where do you live?

M : I live in a two-room apartment on Queen Street.

W : Is it in a big building?

M : Yes. My apartment is on the 19ᵗʰ floor so I have a great view of the mountains.

Question : In what kind of place does the man live?

A. He lives in a palace.　B. He lives in a big building.

C. He lives on the second floor.

* apartment (ə'pɑrtmənt) *n.* 公寓
building ('bɪldɪŋ) *n.* 建築物；大樓
floor (flor) *n.* 樓層　　　view (vju) *n.* 視野
mountain ('maʊntn̩) *n.* 山
kind (kaɪnd) *n.* 種類　　　palace ('pælɪs) *n.* 宮殿

27. (**A**) M: What's the temperature?

W: It's quite cool now — about 20 degrees, but the weather forecast said the high will be 30.

M: Is it supposed to rain?

W: No, it should be sunny today.

Question: At what time did this conversation probably take place?

A. 7:00 a.m.　　　　　B. 2:00 p.m.

C. 6:00 p.m.

* temperature〔'tɛmprətʃɚ〕n. 氣溫
quite〔kwaɪt〕adv. 相當　　cool〔kul〕adj. 涼爽的
degree〔dɪ'gri〕n. 度　　forecast〔'for͵kæst〕n. 預測
high〔haɪ〕n. 最高溫　　suppose〔sə'poz〕v. 認為
be supposed to 應該　　probably〔'prɑbəblɪ〕adv. 可能
take place 發生

28. (**C**) W: Do you need any help?

M: Yes, I'd like to pay for these.

W: I can do that for you. Let's go over to the cash register.

Question: What is the man?

A. He is a cashier.　　　　B. He is a patient.

C. He is a customer.

* *pay for* 付～的費用　　*go over to* 前往～
cash register 收銀機
What is the man? 那男人從事什麼職業？
cashier〔kæ'ʃɪr〕n. 收銀員　　patient〔'peʃənt〕n. 病人
customer〔'kʌstəmɚ〕n. 顧客

29. (**A**)　W : Did you go to the concert last night?

　　　　　M : No, I couldn't.

　　　　　W : Why not?

　　　　　M : It was sold out.

　　　　　Question : Why didn't the boy go to the concert?

　　　　　A. He could not buy a ticket.

　　　　　B. The tickets were too expensive.

　　　　　C. He sold his ticket.

　　　　　* concert (ˈkɑnsɝt) *n.* 音樂會；演唱會
　　　　　　sell out 賣光　　expensive (ɪkˈspɛnsɪv) *adj.* 昂貴的

30. (**C**)　W : Doctor, I have a terrible headache and my throat
　　　　　　　hurts.

　　　　　M : You have a cold, but it's not serious.

　　　　　W : What should I do?

　　　　　M : Drink a lot of water and rest.

　　　　　Question : What does the doctor tell the patient to do?

　　　　　A. Take the rest of the medicine.

　　　　　B. Take the cold seriously.

　　　　　C. Take a rest.

　　　　　* terrible (ˈtɛrəbḷ) *adj.* 嚴重的
　　　　　　headache (ˈhɛdˌek) *n.* 頭痛　　throat (θrot) *n.* 喉嚨
　　　　　　hurt (hɝt) *v.* 疼痛　　*have a cold* 感冒 (= *catch a cold*)
　　　　　　serious (ˈsɪrɪəs) *adj.* 嚴重的　　rest (rɛst) *v. n.* 休息
　　　　　　take (tek) *v.* 吃 (藥)　　*the rest* 剩下的部分
　　　　　　medicine (ˈmɛdəsn̩) *n.* 藥
　　　　　　take ~ seriously 認真看待~　　*take a rest* 休息一下

二、閱讀能力測驗

第一部份：詞彙和結構

1. (**C**) Do some <u>gentle</u> exercise first, or you will hurt yourself.

先做些<u>溫和的</u>運動，否則會傷到自己。

    (A) strict〔strɪkt〕 *adj.* 嚴格的

    (B) natural〔'nætʃərəl〕 *adj.* 自然的

    (C) ***gentle***〔'dʒɛntḷ〕 *adj.* 溫和的

    (D) real〔'riəl〕 *adj.* 真實的

    * exercise〔'ɛksə‚saɪz〕 *n.* 運動   first〔fɝst〕 *adv.* 先
       or〔ɔr〕 *conj.* 否則   hurt〔hɝt〕 *v.* 傷害

2. (**A**) He <u>replied</u> to my question with patience. I'm satisfied with his explanation.

他很有耐心地<u>回答</u>我的問題。我很滿意他的解釋。

    (A) ***reply***〔rɪ'plaɪ〕 *v.* 回答 < *to* >

    (B) answer〔'ænsə〕 *v.* 回答（為及物動詞，不須加 to）

    (C) remember〔rɪ'mɛmbə〕 *v.* 記得

    (D) forget〔fə'gɛt〕 *v.* 忘記

    * patience〔'peʃəns〕 *n.* 耐心
      satisfied〔'sætɪs‚faɪd〕 *adj.* 滿意的 < *with* >
      explanation〔‚ɛksplə'neʃən〕 *n.* 解釋；說明

3. (**D**) As soon as Carrie woke <u>up</u>, she jumped out of bed.

凱莉一<u>醒來</u>，就跳下床。

    wake up 醒來

    * ***as soon as*** 一…就～   jump〔dʒʌmp〕 *v.* 跳
      out of 從…

4. (**B**) Although my grandmother is 95 years old, she is still very <u>healthy</u>. 我祖母雖然今年九十五歲了，但是她仍然非常<u>健康</u>。

  (A) right〔raɪt〕*adj.* 正確的

  (B) *healthy*〔'hɛlθɪ〕*adj.* 健康的

  (C) sick〔sɪk〕*adj.* 生病的

  (D) weak〔wik〕*adj.* 虛弱的

 * grandmother〔'grænd,mʌðɚ〕*n.* 祖母；外婆

  still〔stɪl〕*adv.* 仍然

5. (**A**) Don't bother asking her for help. It would be a <u>waste</u> of time. 不用麻煩請她幫忙。那只是<u>浪費</u>時間。

  (A) *waste*〔west〕*n.* 浪費

  (B) moment〔'moment〕*n.* 片刻

  (C) space〔spes〕*n.* 空位

  (D) hurry〔'hɜɪ〕*n.* 匆忙

 * bother〔'bɑðɚ〕*v.* 麻煩；費事

  ask sb. for sth. 要求某人某物

6. (**B**) Helen's hair is <u>much longer</u> than her sister's.
海倫的頭髮比她姊姊的頭髮<u>長多</u>了。

  由連接詞 than 可知，此為比較級的句型，故 (A) long 不合，選 (B) *much longer*，much 可置於形容詞比較級前面，加強語氣。too 及 very 只能修飾形容詞原級，故 (C) (D) 用法不合。

7. (**B**) Do you mind <u>if</u> I open the window? 你介意我開窗戶嗎？

  Do you mind 習慣接 if 引導的子句，表「如果…，你介不介意？」，用來徵求別人的同意。

8. (**A**) Linda and I are watching <u>our</u> favorite TV program.

琳達和我正在看<u>我們</u>最喜歡的電視節目。

空格應填一所有格，來修飾後面的名詞 favorite TV program，故選 (A) *our*「我們的」。而 (B) ours、(D) hers 為所有格代名詞，(C) we 是主格，用法皆不合。

* program〔'progræm〕 *n.* 節目

9. (**B**) Would you turn <u>up</u> the radio? I'd like to know the news about the typhoon.

你能不能把收音機開<u>大聲</u>點？我想知道颱風的消息。

(A) turn off　關掉（電器）
(B) *turn up*　開大聲
(C) turn in　繳交
(D) turn down　關小聲

* radio〔'redɪ,o〕 *n.* 收音機　　news〔njuz〕 *n.* 新聞
　typhoon〔taɪ'fun〕 *n.* 颱風

10. (**B**) I was busy doing my homework when the phone rang. So I stopped <u>to answer</u> the telephone.

電話響的時候，我正忙著做功課。所以我停下來，<u>去接</u>電話。

stop 的用法：

$$\begin{cases} \text{stop} + \text{V-ing} & \text{停止做} \sim \\ \text{stop} + \text{to V.} & \text{停下來，去做} \sim \end{cases}$$

按照句意，停下手邊的功課，再去接電話，故選 (B) *to answer*。　 *answer the telephone* 接電話

* *be busy* + *V-ing* 忙著　　ring〔rɪŋ〕 *v.*（電話）鈴響

11. (**B**) Without your help, I <u>couldn't</u> have finished my report last night. 如果沒有你的幫忙，昨晚我<u>無法</u>完成報告。

從時間副詞 last night 得知，空格應填過去式助動詞，故 (C)(D) 用法不合，而 (A) shouldn't「不應該」，則不合句意，故選 (B) *couldn't*。could 是 can 的過去式。

* without〔wɪð'aut〕*prep* 如果沒有
finish〔'fɪnɪʃ〕*v.* 完成   report〔rɪ'port〕*n.* 報告

12. (**C**) I can't believe that George is doing the dishes. He <u>hardly</u> does any housework.
我不敢相信喬治正在洗碗。他<u>幾乎不</u>做任何家事的。

按照句意，喬治洗碗是出乎意料之外的事情，故選 (C) *hardly*「幾乎不」，表示他洗碗的頻率很低。而 (A) always「總是」，(B) usually「通常」，(D) finally「最後」，均不合句意。

* believe〔bɪ'liv〕*v.* 相信   *do the dishes* 洗碗
housework〔'haus,wɝk〕*n.* 家事

13. (**A**) Andy : Does Patty go to school early?
Danny : No, she <u>is often</u> late for school.
安迪：派蒂平常很早就到學校嗎？
丹尼：沒有，她上學<u>經常</u>遲到。

often「經常」為頻率副詞，其位置為：

① 一般動詞之前
② be 動詞或助動詞之後
③ 助動詞與一般動詞之間

「be 動詞 + late + for」表「～遲到」，因此動詞須用 be 動詞，選 (A) *is often*。

14. (**D**) Peter and Edward are good friends. They share sorrow and joy with <u>each other</u> all the time.

彼得跟愛德華是好朋友。他們總是<u>互相</u>分享悲傷和喜悅。

each other 互相

而 (A) both「兩者都」,(B) another「(三者以上)另一個」,(C) the other「(兩者中)另一個」,均不合句意。

* share〔ʃɛr〕v. 分享　　sorrow〔'saro〕n. 悲傷
 joy〔dʒɔɪ〕n. 喜悅　　**all the time** 一直;總是

15. (**B**) The waitress <u>serves</u> breakfast at the restaurant every morning, but she didn't work today.

那名女服務生每天早上在餐廳為人<u>供應</u>早餐,但是今天她沒有上班。

由時間副詞 every morning 可知,「早上去餐廳供應早餐」是習慣性的行為,故動詞要用「現在簡單式」,選 (B)。

* waitress〔'wetrɪs〕n. 女服務生
 serve〔sɜv〕v. 端出(食物);供應

第二部份：段落填空

Questions 16-20

This summer I went to New York and stayed with an

American family <u>for</u> two weeks. All the members of the family
        16

were nice <u>to</u> me. During the stay, I noticed several interesting
        17

things about their family life. For example, in my host family,

the father often made dinner for us. He said, " If I helped my

wife <u>with</u> cooking, we can have more time to <u>spend</u> together."
        18   19

The trip gave me an opportunity to see the <u>differences</u> between
                                                            20

the Chinese and American's ways of life.

今年夏天，我到紐約，跟一戶美國家庭住了兩個星期。他們全家人
都對我很好。住在他們家的這段期間，我觀察到他們家庭生活一些有趣
的地方。比如說，這寄宿家庭的父親常煮晚飯給我們吃。他說：「如果
我幫我太太煮飯，我們就有更多時間相處。」這次旅行讓我有機會了解
到，中國與美國生活方式的不同。

stay〔 ste 〕v. n. 暫住　　member〔ˈmɛmbɚ〕n. 成員
notice〔ˈnotɪs〕v. 注意到　　several〔ˈsɛvərəl〕adj. 好幾個
interesting〔ˈɪntrɪstɪŋ〕adj. 有趣的　　*for example* 舉例來說
host〔 host 〕n. 主人　adj. 主人的　　*host family* 寄宿家庭
cooking〔ˈkʊkɪŋ〕n. 煮飯；作菜　　trip〔 trɪp 〕n. 旅行
opportunity〔ˌɑpɚˈtjunətɪ〕n. 機會　　see〔 si 〕v. 知道
way of life 生活方式

16. (**B**) 「for + 一段時間」表「持續~（多久）」。

17. (**C**) *be nice to sb.* 對某人好

18. (**A**) *help sb. with sth.* 幫助某人某事

19. (**A**) (A) *spend* 〔 spɛnd 〕 *v.* 度過（時間）
　　　　　 (B) waste 〔 west 〕 *v.* 浪費
　　　　　 (C) work 〔 wɜk 〕 *v.* 工作
　　　　　 (D) practice 〔ˈpræktɪs 〕 *v.* 練習

20. (**D**) (A) change 〔 tʃendʒ 〕 *n.* 變化
　　　　　 (B) problem 〔ˈprɑbləm 〕 *n.* 問題
　　　　　 (C) language 〔ˈlæŋgwɪdʒ 〕 *n.* 語言
　　　　　 (D) *difference* 〔ˈdɪfrəns 〕 *n.* 差異

Questions 21-25

　　We often see people <u>walking</u> with their dogs. It is still true
　　　　　　　　　　21

that a dog is the most useful <u>animal</u> in the world, but the reason
　　　　　　　　　　　　22

has changed. <u>In</u> the past, dogs were needed to watch doors. But
　　　　　23

now the reason people keep dogs in their houses is that they feel

lonely in the city. For a child, a dog is his or her best friend

when he or she has no friends <u>to play with</u>. For old people, a dog
　　　　　　　　　　　　　24

is also a child when their own children have <u>grown up</u> and left.
　　　　　　　　　　　　　　　　25

People keep dogs as friends, even like members of the family.

　　我們常看到人跟狗走在一起。沒錯，狗對人類而言，仍是全世界最有用的動物，但原因已經改變。以前的狗必須看門。但是現在人們在家養狗的理由，是因為覺得都市生活很寂寞。對小孩而言，沒有朋友可以一起玩時，狗就是他們最好的朋友。對老人而言，如果他們自己的小孩都長大成人，離開家後，狗就像他們的小孩。人們養狗，會把狗當作朋友，甚至當成家人。

useful〔'jusfəl〕adj. 有用的　　in the world 在全世界
reason〔'rizn〕n. 理由；原因　　change〔tʃendʒ〕v. 改變
watch〔watʃ〕v. 看守　　keep〔kip〕v. 飼養
lonely〔'lonlɪ〕adj. 寂寞的　　leave〔liv〕v. 離開
as〔æz〕prep. 當作　　member〔'mɛmbə〕n 成員

21. (**A**) see 為感官動詞，接受詞後，須接原形動詞或現在分詞，故選 (A) *walking*。

22. (**D**) (A) machine〔mə'ʃin〕n. 機器
　　　　　(B) student〔'stjudṇt〕n. 學生
　　　　　(C) room〔rum〕n. 房間
　　　　　(D) *animal*〔'ænəml〕n. 動物

23. (**A**) *in the past* 在過去

24. (**B**) 不定詞片語 *to play with* 做形容詞用，修飾 friends，不可以省略 with，因為本題的 play「玩耍」是不及物動詞。

$$\begin{cases} \cdots\text{he or she has no friends } \textit{to play with}. \\ = \cdots\text{he or she has no friends } \textit{that they can play with}. \end{cases}$$

25. (**D**) (A) shut up 閉嘴　　(B) get up 起床
　　　　　(C) stand up 起立　　(D) *grow up* 長大

第三部份：閱讀理解

Question 26

請在紅線後等待

behind〔bɪˋhaɪnd〕*prep.* 在…之後（= *in back of*）
line〔laɪn〕*n.* 線；（等待順序的）行列；（電話）線路

26.（**C**）此告示牌是什麼意思？
　　(A) 排隊等候。　　　　　(B) 電話忙線中。
　　(C) 站在此線後面。　　　(D) 不要掛電話。
　　* sign〔saɪn〕*n.* 告示牌　　mean〔min〕*v.* 意思是
　　busy〔ˋbɪzɪ〕*adj.*（電話）忙線中

Questions 27-28

芮妮林
通化街 200 巷 11 號
台灣，台北市 106 大安區
中華民國

　　　　　　　　史考特・布朗先生
　　　　　　　　拉斯維加斯大道 3200 號
　　　　　　　　拉斯維加斯，內華達州 89109
航空郵件　　　美國

No.　號碼（－*number*）　　lane〔len〕*n.* 巷

St.　街（＝*street*）　　R.O.C. 中華民國（＝*Republic of China*）

Blvd. 林蔭大道（＝boulevard〔ˈbulə͵vɑrd〕）

Las Vegas 拉斯維加斯（美國內華達州的城市）

NV 內華達州（＝Nevada〔nəˈvædə〕）　　*air mail* 航空郵件

27.（**A**）　這封信是誰寫的？

　　　　（A）芮妮。　　　　　　　　（B）大安區。

　　　　（C）通化街。　　　　　　　（D）史考特。

　　　　* 美式信封上，寄信人的姓名及地址寫在左上角。

28.（**C**）　這封信要寄到哪一個城市？

　　　　（A）台北市。　　　　　　　（B）台灣。

　　　　（C）拉斯維加斯。　　　　　（D）美國。

　　　　* 美式信封上，收信人的姓名及地址寫在中央。

Questions 29-30

準備好了嗎？

你迫不急待想向別人秀出你有多棒嗎？你有非常棒的歌喉嗎？你樂器玩得很好嗎？或者你有任何特殊才藝嗎？最重要的是，你想在捷運站秀出你自己嗎？台北捷運公司徵求街頭藝人。來參加選拔大賽，讓我們知道你有多棒！

日期：九月十五日，星期天

時間：上午十點

地點：台北捷運站劇場

---

ready〔ˈrɛdɪ〕adj. 準備好的;樂意的

cannot wait to + V. 迫不及待要~　　show〔ʃo〕v. 給~看

wonderful〔ˈwʌndɚfəl〕adj. 很棒的　　voice〔vɔɪs〕n. 聲音

musical instrument 樂器 (= instrument〔ˈɪnstrəmənt〕)

talent〔ˈtælənt〕n. 才華　　***most important of all*** 最重要的是

show off 賣弄;炫耀　　***MRT*** 捷運 (= *Mass Rapid Transit*)

station〔ˈsteʃən〕n. 車站　　rapid〔ˈræpɪd〕adj. 快速的

transit〔ˈtræsɪt〕n. 公共交通運輸系統

corporation〔ˌkɔrpəˈreʃən〕n. 公司　　***look for*** 尋找

performer〔pɚˈfɔrmɚ〕n. 表演者

street performer 街頭藝人　　tryout〔ˈtraɪˌaut〕n. 選拔賽

date〔det〕n. 日期　　theater〔ˈθiətɚ〕n. 劇場

main〔men〕adj. 主要的;最重要的

Taipei Main Station 台北捷運站

29. (**D**) 台北捷運公司希望人們做什麼?

(A) 多搭乘捷運。　　　　　　(B) 每當搭捷運時要秀自己。

(C) 在捷運上歌唱課。　　　　(D) <u>在捷運站表演。</u>

* ride〔raɪd〕v. 搭乘　　whenever〔hwɛnˈɛvɚ〕conj. 每當

take a lesson 上課　　perform〔pɚˈfɔrm〕v. 表演

30. (**D**) 哪個字和 "tryout" 的意思最接近?

(A) 運動練習。　　　　　　　(B) 全班旅行。

(C) 駕訓課。　　　　　　　　(D) <u>試演。</u>

* close〔klos〕adj. 接近的　　meaning〔ˈminɪŋ〕n. 意思

sports〔sports〕adj. 運動的

practice〔ˈpræktɪs〕n. 練習

driving〔ˈdraɪvɪŋ〕adj. 駕駛的　　test〔tɛst〕n. 試驗

performance〔pɚˈfɔrməns〕n. 演出

Questions 31-33

Last week I went to visit my friend Emily in the hospital. She had her appendix taken out. She had to be hospitalized for 10 days. The doctor told her that she wouldn't be allowed to do any sports for a while. You can imagine that Emily felt very unhappy. Some of us shared the cost of a big stuffed teddy bear. We bought it for her to cheer her up. When she saw it, she started to laugh. Then she shouted, "Ouch! Ouch! Ow!" Poor Emily, I asked her if she was in pain. She answered, "Only when I laugh, Barbara. Only when I laugh."

上星期，我去醫院探望我的朋友愛蜜莉。她動手術切除盲腸。她必須住院住十天。醫生告訴她，這一陣子不可以做運動。你可以想像愛蜜莉有多不開心。我們一些人一起出錢，買了一隻很大的泰迪熊。我們買泰迪熊是爲了讓她開心。當她看到泰迪熊的時候，她開始大笑。然後她大叫：「哎喲！哎喲！噢！」可憐的愛蜜莉，我問她會不會痛。她說：「只有在笑的時候才會，芭芭拉。只有在笑的時候。」

visit〔ˈvɪzɪt〕v. 探望　　hospital〔ˈhɑspɪtl̩〕n. 醫院

appendix〔əˈpɛndɪks〕n. 盲腸　　*take out* 取出

hospitalize〔ˈhɑspɪtl̩ˌaɪz〕v. 使住院治療

allow〔əˈlau〕v. 允許　　while〔hwaɪl〕n. 一會兒；一段時間

imagine〔ɪˈmædʒɪn〕v. 想像

unhappy〔ʌnˈhæpɪ〕adj. 不愉快的　　share〔ʃɛr〕v. 分攤

cost〔kɔst〕n. 費用　　stuffed〔stʌft〕adj. 填充玩具的

teddy bear 泰迪熊　　*cheer up* 使高興

start〔stɑrt〕v. 開始　　laugh〔læf〕v. 笑

shout〔ʃaut〕v. 大叫　　ouch〔autʃ〕interj. 哎喲！（突然疼痛時

　發出的聲音，等於 ow〔au〕）　　poor〔pur〕adj. 可憐的

pain〔pen〕n. 疼痛　　*be in pain* 在痛苦中

31. (**C**) 從本文，我們可以知道關於愛蜜莉的什麼事情？

(A) 她希望將來能成爲醫生。

(B) 她一點都不喜歡泰迪熊。

(C) <u>她喜歡運動。</u>

(D) 她經常待在醫院。

* *in the future* 在未來　　*not…at all* 一點也不

sport〔sport〕*n.* 運動　　*play sports* 運動 (= *do sports*)

32. (**B**) 愛蜜莉爲什麼要去醫院？

(A) 她在醫院工作。

(B) <u>她必須動手術。</u>

(C) 她想要探望一位生病的朋友。

(D) 她不想上學。

* operation〔ˌɑpəˈreʃən〕*n.* 手術

33. (**B**) 愛蜜莉可能何時可以再運動？

(A) 一把盲腸割掉後。

(B) <u>再過幾個禮拜。</u>

(C) 當她加入醫院團隊後。

(D) 再過九天。

* *be able to* + *V.* 能夠　　*as soon as* 一…就～

join〔dʒɔɪn〕*v.* 加入　　team〔tim〕*n.* 團隊

Questions 34-35

最近五天的氣象預報

今天	明天	星期五	星期六	星期天
雲量偏多	多雲	多雲	雲量偏多	多雲
最高溫：32	最高溫：35	最高溫：33	最高溫：35	最高溫：29
最低溫：25	最低溫：27	最低溫：25	最低溫：25	最低溫：23

weather (ˈwɛðɚ) n. 天氣　　forecast (ˈforˌkæst) n. 預報
mostly (ˈmostlɪ) adv. 大部分地；主要地
cloudy (ˈklaʊdɪ) adj. 多雲的
high (haɪ) n. 最高溫　　low (lo) n. 最低溫

34. (**B**)　這個星期的天氣如何？

(A) 下雨。　　　　　　(B) 多雲。
(C) 晴朗。　　　　　　(D) 下雪。

* rainy (ˈrenɪ) adj. 下雨的
　 sunny (ˈsʌnɪ) adj. 晴朗的
　 snowy (ˈsnoɪ) adj. 下雪的

35. (**C**) 下列敘述何者正確？

    (A) 星期六的夜間氣溫將是這星期最高的。

    (B) 星期天將是這星期最溫暖的一天。

    (C) <u>明天氣溫會上升。</u>

    (D) 星期六將是這星期雲量最多的一天。

    * nighttime〔'naɪt,taɪm〕*adj.* 夜間的
      temperature〔'tɛmprətʃɚ〕*n.* 氣溫
      warm〔wɔrm〕*adj.* 溫暖的   ***go up*** 上升；增加

三、寫作能力測驗

第一部份：單句寫作

第1～5題：句子改寫

1. I asked Amy, "Could you pass me some napkins?"

  I asked Amy if _____ pass me some napkins.

    重點結構：直接問句改為間接問句的用法

      解   答：<u>I asked Amy if she could pass me some</u>
             <u>napkins.</u>

    句型分析：I asked Amy + if + 主詞 + 動詞

      說   明：Could you pass me some napkins? 是直接問句，
             現在要放在 if（是否）後面，做為 I asked Amy 的
             受詞，即名詞子句（間接問句）「連接詞＋主詞＋
             動詞」的形式，在 I asked Amy 後面接 if she could
             pass me some napkins，並把問號改成句點。

    * pass〔pæs〕*v.* 傳遞   napkin〔'næpkɪn〕*n.* 餐巾紙

2. Helen seldom rides a bike home.

_____ _____ last month.

重點結構：過去式動詞

　解　答：Helen seldom rode a bike home last month.

句型分析：主詞 + 動詞 + 時間副詞

　說　明：時間副詞為 last month，故動詞要改為過去式，
　　　　　rides 改成 rode。

* seldom (ˋsɛldəm) adv. 很少　　bike (baɪk) n. 腳踏車

3. Lisa and her cousin played table tennis.

When _____?

重點結構：wh-問句的用法

　解　答：When did Lisa and her cousin play table tennis?

句型分析：When + 助動詞 + 主詞 + 動詞 ?

　說　明：played 為過去式動詞，故助動詞用 did，主詞後的
　　　　　動詞須用原形動詞 play。

* cousin (ˋkʌzn̩) n. 堂（表）兄弟姊妹　　*table tennis* 桌球

4. John : Did you go to the library to return my books?
　Nick : Oh, I forgot.
　Nick forgot _____ to return John's books.

重點結構：「forget + to V.」的用法

　解　答：Nick forgot to go to the library to return
　　　　　John's books.

句型分析：主詞 + forget + to V.

　說　明：「忘記去做某件事」用 forget + to V. 來表示，
　　　　　此題須在 forgot 後面接不定詞。

* library (ˋlaɪ͵brɛrɪ) n. 圖書館　　return (rɪˋtɝn) v. 歸還

5. To go traveling in Africa is my dream.
   It's _____.

  重點結構：以 It 為虛主詞引導的句子

   解 答：It's my dream to go traveling in Africa.

  句型分析：It's + 形容詞 + to V.

   說 明：虛主詞 It 代替不定詞片語，真正的主詞是不定詞
       片語 to go traveling in Africa，放在句尾。

  * **go traveling** 去旅行 Africa〔'æfrɪkə〕n. 非洲
  dream〔drim〕n. 夢想

第 6～10 題：句子合併

6. Laura asked Linda something.
   The computer didn't work.
   Laura asked Linda why _____.

  重點結構：名詞子句當受詞用

   解 答：Laura asked Linda why the computer didn't work.

  句型分析：Laura asked Linda + why + 主詞 + 動詞

   說 明：題目中，蘿拉要問琳達一件事，就是關於電腦不能
       用這件事，兩句之間用疑問詞 why 來合併，如果
       是直接問句的話，我們會說："Why didn't the
       computer work?"，但這裡前面有 Laura asked
       Linda，因此後面必須接名詞子句，做為受詞，即
       「疑問詞 + 主詞 + 動詞」的形式，在 Laura asked
       Linda 後面接 why the computer didn't work。

  * computer〔kəm'pjutə〕n. 電腦
  work〔wɝk〕v.（機器）運轉

7. You can play video games.

You finish your homework.

You ___ _____ as long as _____.

重點結構：as long as 的用法

解　答：<u>You can play video games as long as you finish</u>
<u>your homework.</u>

句型分析：主詞＋動詞＋as long as＋主詞＋動詞

説　明：這題的句意是「你可以打電動玩具，只要你把功課做
完。」as long as「只要」爲連接詞片語，故後面要
接完整的子句，即主詞加動詞的形式。

＊ *video game* 電動玩具　　*as long as* 只要

8. Patricia takes a shower.

Then, she has dinner.

Patricia ___ _____ after _____.

重點結構：after 的用法

解　答：<u>Patricia has dinner after she takes a shower.</u>
或 <u>Patricia has dinner after (taking) a shower.</u>

句型分析：主詞＋動詞＋before＋主詞＋動詞
　　　　　或 主詞＋動詞＋before＋（動）名詞

説　明：then「然後」表示派翠西亞先洗澡，再吃晚餐，現
在用 after「在～之後」來表示事情的先後順序。而
after 有兩種詞性，若作爲連接詞，引導副詞子句
時，須接完整的主詞與動詞，即 after she takes a
shower；若作爲介系詞，後面須接名詞或動名詞，
即 after a shower 或 after taking a shower。

＊ *take a shower* 淋浴　　 have〔hæv〕 *v.* 吃

9. Gail cleans the classroom.

David helps her.

David helps Gail _____.

　重點結構：「help + *sb.* + (to) V.」的用法

　　解　答：David helps Gail (to) clean the classroom.

　句型分析：help + 受詞 + 不定詞或原形動詞

　　説　明：這題的意思是「大衛幫蓋兒打掃教室」，help 的用法是接受詞後，須接不定詞，不定詞的 to 也可省略。

　　* clean〔klin〕*v.* 打掃

10. I will go to the supermarket tomorrow.

I'll mail the letter for you.

I'll mail the letter for you when _____ tomorrow.

　重點結構：未來式的 wh-問句

　　解　答：I'll mail the letter for you when I go to the supermarket tomorrow.

　句型分析：I'll mail the letter for you + when + 主詞 + 動詞

　　説　明：在表時間的副詞子句中，要用現在式代替未來式，所以雖然「我明天將去超級市場」是未來的時間，但不能造 when I *will go* to the supermarket tomorrow，須用 when I *go* to the supermarket tomorrow。

　　* supermarket〔'supɚ,markɪt〕*n.* 超級市場

　　　mail〔mel〕*v.* 郵寄　　letter〔'lɛtɚ〕*n.* 信

第 11~15 題：重組

11. How many ＿＿＿＿＿＿＿＿＿＿＿＿＿＿＿＿＿＿＿?
    does / have / grandchildren / Vincent

　　重點結構：「How many + 複數名詞？」的用法
　　解　答：<u>How many grandchildren does Vincent have?</u>
　　句型分析：How many + 複數名詞 + 助動詞 + 主詞 + 動詞
　　說　明：「How many + 複數名詞？」表「~有(多少)？」。
　　* grandchildren〔'grænd,tʃɪldrən〕*n. pl.* 孫子(女)

12. My ＿＿＿＿＿＿＿＿＿＿＿＿＿＿＿＿＿＿＿.
    goes / work / MRT / usually / by / to / father

　　重點結構：usually 的用法
　　解　答：<u>My father usually goes to work by MRT.</u>
　　句型分析：主詞 + usually + 一般動詞
　　說　明：usually 為頻率副詞，須置於一般動詞的前面。
　　　　　　　而「by + 交通工具」表「搭乘~」，置於句尾。

13. Swimming ＿＿＿＿＿＿＿＿＿＿＿＿＿＿＿＿＿.
    one / is / favorite / sports / my / of

　　重點結構：「one of + 所有格 + 複數名詞」的用法
　　解　答：<u>Swimming is one of my favorite sports.</u>
　　句型分析：主詞 + be 動詞 + one of + 所有格 + 複數名詞
　　說　明：本題是說「游泳是我最喜愛的運動之一」，「~當中
　　　　　　　的一個」用「one of + 複數名詞」來表示。

14. Mr. Kelly _____.

worked / has / for / in / years / elementary school / the / three

　　重點結構：現在完成式字序

　　　解　答：<u>Mr. Kelly has worked in the elementary school</u>
　　　　　　　<u>for three years.</u>

　　句型分析：主詞 + have/has + 過去分詞 + for + 一段時間

　　　說　明：現在完成式的結構是「主詞 + have/has + 過去
　　　　　　　分詞」，而「for + 一段時間」，表「持續（多
　　　　　　　久）」，此時間片語須置於句尾。

　　* **elementary school** 小學

15. This _____.

most / have / building / I / is / beautiful / the / ever / seen

　　重點結構：形容詞最高級的用法

　　　解　答：<u>This is the most beautiful building I have ever</u>
　　　　　　　<u>seen.</u>

　　句型分析：the most + 形容詞

　　　說　明：beautiful 為兩個音節以上的形容詞，故前面加
　　　　　　　most，形成最高級。I have ever seen 作形容詞
　　　　　　　子句，修飾 building。

　　* building (ˈbɪldɪŋ) n. 建築物

第二部份：段落寫作

題目：昨天媽媽過生日，你和弟弟一起去買禮物，最後挑了一支手錶
送給媽媽，請根據圖片內容寫一篇約 50 字的簡短描述。

Yesterday was my mother's birthday. My brother and I
went to a department store to buy a gift. We wanted to buy
some beautiful clothes, but we did not see anything we liked.
In the end, we bought her a new watch. It is very fashionable.
Last night we had a birthday party. We sang and ate cake.
We also gave our mother the present. She was very happy.

>***department store*** 百貨公司
>gift〔gɪft〕*n.* 禮物（＝*present*）　　***in the end*** 最後
>fashionable〔'fæʃənəbḷ〕*adj.* 流行的；時髦的
>***have a birthday party*** 舉行生日派對

心得筆記欄

全民英語能力分級檢定測驗
初級測驗④

一、聽力測驗

　　本測驗分三部份，全爲三選一之選擇題，每部份各 10 題，共 30 題，作答時間約 20 分鐘。

第一部份 · 看圖辨義

　　本部份共 10 題，試題冊上每題有一個圖片，請聽錄音機播出一個相關的問題，與 A、B、C 三個英語敘述後，選一個與所看到圖片最相符的答案，並在答案紙上相對的圓圈內塗黑作答。每題播出一遍，問題及選項均不印在試題冊上。

例：(看)

NT$80　　NT$50

(聽)

Look at the picture. How much is the hamburger?

　　A.　It's eighty dollars.
　　B.　It's fifty-five dollars.
　　C.　It's eighteen dollars.

正確答案爲 A

Question 1

Question 2

Question 3

Question 4

Question 5

Question 6

請翻頁 ⇒

Question 7

Question 8

Question 9

Question 10

請翻頁 ⫸

第二部份：問答

本部份共 10 題，每題錄音機會播出一個問句或直述句，
每題播出一次，聽後請從試題冊上 A、B、C 三個選項中，
選出一個最適合的回答或回應，並在答案紙上塗黑作答。

例：

（聽）　Good morning, Kevin. How are you?

（看）　A.　I'm fine, thank you.
　　　　B.　I'm in the living room.
　　　　C.　My name is Kevin.

正確答案為 A

11. A. Yes, I do.
　　B. No, I haven't.
　　C. I always don't.

12. A. I don't know the answer.
　　B. All right.
　　C. No, thank you.

13. A. Oh, you shouldn't have.
　　B. It looks great.
　　C. Where should I pay it?

14. A. I enjoy movies very much.
　　B. It was so-so.
　　C. I'd love to.

15. A. Let's play basketball.
    B. I was taking a walk.
    C. I always do it there.

16. A. I like him.
    B. I think he is new, too.
    C. I don't think we will
       have a new teacher
       this year.

17. A. The basketball game
       on Channel 4.
    B. The novel *Harry Potter*.
    C. The radio.

18. A. Same to you.
    B. I have one, thank
       you.
    C. No, I haven't.

19. A. Yes, it will.
    B. No, not very many.
    C. Yes, a little.

20. A. We played two
       games.
    B. It was a tie.
    C. I want to play.

請 翻 頁 ◀▭━▷

第三部份：簡短對話

本部份共 10 題，每題錄音機會播出一段對話及一個相關的問題，每題播出兩次，聽後請從試題冊上 A、B、C 三個選項中，選出一個最適合的回答，並在答案紙上塗黑作答。

例：

（聽）(Woman) Good afternoon, ...Mr. Davis?

(Man) Yes. I have an appointment with Dr. Sanders at two o'clock. My son Tommy has a fever.

(Woman) Oh, that's too bad. Well, please have a seat, Mr. Davis. Dr. Sanders will be right with you.

Question: Where did this conversation take place?

（看）A. In a post office.

B. In a restaurant.

C. In a doctor's office.

正確答案為 C

21. A. A test.

B. A report.

C. A history book.

22. A. Hungry.

B. Thirsty.

C. Sick.

23. A. He doesn't like any team at all.
    B. He likes every team the same amount.
    C. He is a Tigers fan.

24. A. The first grade of elementary school.
    B. Seventh grade.
    C. The first grade of senior high school.

25. A. The boy deserved to pass the exam because he worked hard.
    B. It is surprising that the boy passed the exam.
    C. The boy should have studied harder for the exam.

26. A. A bus ticket.
    B. 100 dollars in change.
    C. Fifteen dollars.

27. A. What time the program will start.
    B. What to watch on television.
    C. Where their mother is.

28. A. He bought the jacket at a low price.
    B. He wants to sell his jacket.
    C. He would rather have an expensive jacket.

29. A. He called the wrong number.
    B. He talked to Monica.
    C. He lied to Monica.

30. A. He lost it.
    B. He spent it all on drinking coffee.
    C. He used it to play on-line games.

請翻頁 ▯⟹

二、閱讀能力測驗

本測驗分三部份，全爲四選一之選擇題，共 35 題，作答時間 35 分鐘。

第一部份：詞彙和結構

本部份共 15 題，每題含一個空格。請就試題冊上 A、B、C、D 四個選項中選出最適合題意的字或詞，標示在答案紙上。

1. Betty wants to be an _____ because drawing is her passion.
   A. artist
   B. scientist
   C. pianist
   D. guitarist

2. All the guests thought the wedding was important, so they were all dressed in _____ clothes.
   A. fluent
   B. formal
   C. funny
   D. flat

3. Brenda didn't take the computer class because she couldn't _____ up her mind.
   A. take
   B. change
   C. build
   D. make

4. My _____ is that he didn't come because his parents wouldn't let him. I'm not sure.
   A. plan
   B. truth
   C. knowledge
   D. guess

5. To _____ my father's birthday, we are going to the mountains for a two-day vacation.
   A. treat
   B. celebrate
   C. collect
   D. allow

6 _____ you take a modern history class next semester?
   A. Did
   B. Have
   C. Can
   D. Are

7. I'm afraid _____ our neighbor's big dog.
   A. by
   B. to
   C. of
   D. with

請 翻 頁 ⟦⟹

8. Chinese New Year is coming, and all the people are busy _____ their houses.

   A. clean
   B. to clean
   C. cleaning
   D. to cleaning

9. Go two blocks, _____ you'll see the bookstore.

   A. and
   B. or
   C. because
   D. so

10. Leo has quit smoking. He doesn't smoke _____.

   A. again
   B. anymore
   C. anywhere
   D. anyway

11. Last night, it took me almost three hours _____ for the science test.

   A. to preparing
   B. preparing
   C. to prepare
   D. prepare

12. Two cute pandas came to Taiwan _____ last September.
    A. on
    B. in
    C. at
    D. ×

13. We have a cat _____ color is black and white.
    A. who
    B. which
    C. whose
    D. that

14. My sister wants a motorcycle, but she has no money to buy _____.
    A. the one
    B. one
    C. it
    D. the other

15. English is _____ to me that I take every opportunity to practice it.
    A. so interested
    B. very interested
    C. so interesting
    D. very interesting

請 翻 頁 ⫸

第二部份：段落填空

本部份共 10 題，包括二個段落，每個段落各含 5 個空格。
請就試題冊上 A、B、C、D 四個選項中選出最適合題意
的字或詞，標示在答案紙上。

Questions 16-20

Billy had a terrible day today. First, he ___(16)___ up by a
strange call ___(17)___ three o'clock this morning. When he was
going to pick up the receiver, the phone stopped ___(18)___. Then,
he overslept and ___(19)___ the school bus, so he was thirty
minutes late for school. His teacher was very angry. What was
___(20)___, when he got home this afternoon, he couldn't open
the door because he had left his keys in the classroom.

16. A. was woken
    B. is woken
    C. wakes
    D. woke

17. A. at
    B. in
    C. ×
    D. on

18. A. ring
    B. to ring
    C. ringing
    D. and rang

19. A. left
    B. lost
    C. caught
    D. missed

20. A. worse
    B. poorer
    C. angrier
    D. later

Questions 21-25

Do you know what to do in an earthquake? When there is an earthquake, many things can fall down on you. So if you are inside, find a ___(21)___ place such as under a table or in a doorway. If you are ___(22)___ , go to an open area and ___(23)___ your head. If you are driving a car, stop the car at the side of the road and ___(24)___ . Stay in your safe place until the shaking stops. You cannot stop an earthquake, but you can be ___(25)___ for one.

21. A. quiet
    B. noisy
    C. safe
    D. dangerous

22. A. outside
    B. inside
    C. outdoor
    D. indoor

23. A. cover
    B. to cover
    C. covering
    D. to covering

24. A. walk
    B. run
    C. jump
    D. wait

25. A. nervous
    B. ready
    C. surprised
    D. impressed

請 翻 頁 ▯⟹

第三部份： 閱讀理解

本部份共10題，包括數段短文，每段短文後有1～3個相關問題，請就試題冊上A、B、C、D四個選項中選出最適合者，標示在答案紙上。

Questions 26-28

BOOK GARDEN
GRAND OPENING

Book Garden has finally arrived in Taiwan! Don't miss our Grand Opening celebration, starting next Saturday! For two weeks only, you'll enjoy savings of 20 to 40 percent on all of your favorite books. This is the place that has the largest selection of books on the island — fiction, drama, poetry, real-life stories, magazines, and more.

🎁 *Be our 1000th customer, and win great presents.*

26. What is Book Garden celebrating for?

   A. It is going to close business.

   B. It is celebrating its 30th birthday.

   C. It is opening its 1000th store in the world.

   D. It is opening its first store in Taiwan.

27. How long will the sale last?

   A. A weekend.

   B. Fourteen days.

   C. A week.

   D. A month.

28. According to the advertisement, what does Book Garden
   NOT promise to do during the sale?

   A. Deliver books free.

   B. Offer many different kinds of books.

   C. Lower its prices.

   D. Give gifts to its one-thousandth customer.

請 翻 頁 ⫸

Questions 29-30

Here are the contents of six lessons in a book. Read it carefully and answer the questions.

Lesson One	I Love E-Mail ✗✗✗✗✗✗✗✗✗✗	1
Lesson Two	Healthy Diet ✗✗✗✗✗✗✗✗✗✗✗	16
Lesson Three	Lose Weight Easily ✗✗✗✗✗✗	28
Lesson Four	Talking with Your Hands ✗✗	40
Lesson Five	Future World ✗✗✗✗✗✗✗✗✗✗	58
Lesson Six	Believe It or Not ✗✗✗✗✗✗✗✗	70

29. People who cannot **speak** can move their fingers to tell others what they want to say. Joseph wants to know more about it. Which lesson is useful for him?
    A. Lesson One.
    B. Lesson Two.
    C. Lesson Three.
    D. Lesson Four.

30. Which of the following is **NOT** true?

    A. Lesson One is about computers.

    B. Lesson Five is longer than Lesson One.

    C. Maybe there are strange stories in the last lesson.

    D. People who wants to go on a diet should read Lesson Two and Lesson Three.

Question 31

31. What does this sign mean?

    A. No parking.

    B. Fasten your seat belt.

    C. Do not enter.

    D. Exit.

請翻頁 ▐◯⟹

Questions 32-33

March 1, 2003

Dear son,

How are you? It's just one month since I came to Canada. I'm learning English after work because I need to talk to people around me in English.

Last night, my English teacher, Mr. Smith, said to me, "You look tired. How come, Mr. Liu?" I said, "How…come…? Well, I…I…I come here by subway." The teacher said, "I know you come here by subway, but how come you are tired?" I didn't understand him well and didn't say anything. Then he smiled and said, "Well, I am asking why you are tired."

I know both "how" and "come," but I didn't understand "How come?" It was really new to me. Have you learned it at school? English is interesting, isn't it? Every day I'm learning new things in this way. I have had a lot of wonderful experience. How about you?

I hope to hear from you soon.

With love,
Dad

32. Which of the following is true?

    A. This is a letter from a daughter to her father.

    B. Mr. Liu was tired because he worked for Metro.

    C. Mr. Liu came to Canada in the beginning of February.

    D. Mr. Liu works after his English class.

33. What does it mean if Mr. Smith asks Mr. Liu, "How come you are late?"

    A. How do you come late?

    B. Why are you late?

    C. Why not are you late?

    D. How are you late?

請 翻 頁 ◀▯◀▯⟹

Questions 34-35

I had a funny dream last night. I dreamed that I became Superman. I was smart and strong. I had the best grades in my class. I was good at playing basketball, baseball and volleyball. At the same time, I was the captain of all three school teams.

After school, I wore Superman clothing and helped people in need. I helped an old lady cross the road and a little girl take her kite down from a tree. I also helped the police catch bad people. I did so many good things that the President invited me to have dinner. But I didn't accept his invitation because I had to study for my final exam. What a strange ending my dream had!

34. What did the writer dream last night?
   A. He was Superman.
   B. He bumped into Superman.
   C. Superman helped him.
   D. Superman taught him how to make good shots in basketball games.

35. In the writer's dream, what did he do after school?
   A. He gave his seat to a policeman on the bus.
   B. He helped a little girl to take her kite down from a tree.
   C. He had dinner with the President.
   D. He forgot what happened at the end of his dream.

三、寫作能力測驗

本測驗共有兩部份,第一部份為單句寫作,第二部份為段落寫作。
測驗時間為 40 分鐘。

第一部份: 單句寫作
請將答案寫在寫作能力測驗答案紙對應的題號旁,如有拼
字、標點、大小寫之錯誤,將予扣分。

第 1～5 題: 句子改寫
請依題目之提示,將原句改寫成指定型式,並將改寫的句
子完整地寫在答案紙上(包括提示之文字及標點符號)。

1. She wrote this famous novel.

   This famous novel _____ her.

2. Listening to popular music is fun.

   It's _____.

3. When will the next bus come?

   I'd like to know when _____.

4. Nicolas went home after school.

   Where _____ after school?

5. My friend gave me a stuffed doll.

   My friend _____ me.

請 翻 頁 ⮕

第 6～10 題：句子合併

請依照題目指示，將兩句合併成一句，並將合併的句子
完整地寫在答案紙上（包括提示之文字及標點符號）。

6. Don't drink too much coffee.
   You will not fall asleep easily.

   Don't drink too much coffee, _____.

7. We had a music class this morning.
   We had a PE class this morning.

   We had both a music _____ this morning.

8. The rain is very heavy.
   Tammy cannot drive safely.

   The rain is too heavy for Tammy _____.

9. A cup of coffee costs 50 dollars.
   A cup of tea costs 60 dollars.

   A cup of tea is _____ than a cup of coffee.

10. Ron is very old.
    He can drive a car.

    Ron is old enough _____.

第 11～15 題：重組

　　請將題目中所有提示字詞整合成一有意義的句子，並
　　將重組的句子完整地寫在答案紙上（包括提示之文字
　　及標點符號）。答案中必須使用所有提示字詞，且不
　　能隨意增加字詞，否則不予計分。

11. Caroline _____ _____.
    couldn't sleep / that / nervous / she / so / was

12. Neither I ___ _____.
    can / sister / my / nor / cook

13. I asked Mother _____.
    at the station / she / pick me up / could / if

14. Jenny _____.
    Nicolas / a pen / his birthday / sent / for

15. _____, please?
    paper / you / me / another / Could / give

第二部份: 段落寫作

題目: 昨天你和朋友坐捷運到動物園,看到你最喜歡的動物——企鵝
（penguins）,請根據圖片內容寫一篇約 50 字的簡短描述。

_____

_____

_____

_____

_____

_____

初級英檢模擬試題④詳解

一、聽力測驗

Look at the picture for question 1.

1. (**B**) What did he spill?

    A. "Oh, no!"

    B. His coffee.

    C. On the chair.

    * spill〔spɪl〕v. 灑出　　coffee〔'kɔfɪ〕n. 咖啡

Look at the picture for question 2.

2. (**C**) Where are the shorts?

    A. It is windy.

    B. In the sky.

    C. On the ground.

    * shorts〔ʃɔrts〕n. pl. 短褲

    windy〔'wɪndɪ〕adj. 多風的

    sky〔skaɪ〕n. 天空　　ground〔graʊnd〕n. 地面

Look at the picture for question 3.

3. (**B**) Why is he in bed?

    A. It is night.

    B. He is sick.

    C. It is six o'clock.

    * *in bed* 躺在床上　　sick〔sɪk〕adj. 生病的

Look at the picture for question 4.

4. (**A**) What is he doing?

    A. He is staying up late.

    B. He is tired.

    C. He has a test.

    * ***stay up*** 熬夜   late〔let〕*adv.* 晚
    tired〔taɪrd〕*adj.* 疲倦的   test〔tɛst〕*n.* 考試

Look at the picture for question 5.

5. (**B**) What does the man sell?

    A. He has a notebook.

    B. He has umbrellas.

    C. He is running.

    * sell〔sɛl〕*v.* 賣   notebook〔'not,bʊk〕*n.* 筆記本
    umbrella〔ʌm'brɛlə〕*n.* 雨傘

Look at the picture for question 6.

6. (**B**) What are they?

    A. A ring.

    B. Newlyweds.

    C. A wedding.

    * ***What are they?*** 他們是誰？   ring〔rɪŋ〕*n.* 戒指
    newlyweds〔'njulɪ,wɛdz〕*n. pl.* 新婚夫婦
    wedding〔'wɛdɪŋ〕*n.* 婚禮

Look at the picture for question 7.

7. (**C**) What does the girl want?

    A. She wants to sell the dress.

    B. She wants to pay 90 dollars.

    C. She wants a discount.

    * sell (sɛl) v. 賣   dress (drɛs) n. 洋裝
      pay (pe) v. 付   discount ('dɪskaʊnt) n. 折扣

Look at the picture for question 8.

8. (**A**) What happened to the girl?

    A. She dropped the bag.

    B. She found some new clothes.

    C. She washed the clothes.

    * *happen to* 發生   drop (drɑp) v. 使掉落
      clothes (kloðz) n. pl. 衣服   wash (wɑʃ) v. 洗

Look at the picture for question 9.

9. (**A**) Where are his glasses?

    A. They are on the floor.

    B. They are broken.

    C. He cannot see well.

    * glasses ('glæsɪz) n. pl. 眼鏡
      floor (flor) n. 地板
      broken ('brokən) adj. 破碎的
      see well 看得很清楚

Look at the picture for question 10.

10. (**C**) What is she eating?

    A. It is ten to seven.

    B. She is hungry.

    C. It is breakfast.

    * ***It is ten to seven.*** 現在差十分就七點；現在是六點五十分。

    hungry〔'hʌŋgrɪ〕*adj.* 飢餓的

第二部份

11. (**A**) Do you always have to take the bus to school?

    A. Yes, I do.

    B. No, I haven't.

    C. I always don't.

    * always〔'ɔlwez〕*adv.* 總是   ***have to*** 必須

12. (**B**) The phone is ringing. Please answer it.

    A. I don't know the answer.

    B. All right.

    C. No, thank you.

    * phone〔fon〕*n.* 電話 (= *telephone*)

    ring〔rɪŋ〕*v.* (鈴)響

    answer〔'ænsə〕*v.* 接(電話) *n.* 答案

    All right. 好的。

13. (**C**) Here is your bill, sir.

A. Oh, you shouldn't have.

B. It looks great.

C. Where should I pay it?

* bill〔bɪl〕*n.* 帳單　　sir〔sɝ〕*n.*【稱呼】先生
You shouldn't have. 你不用這麼做的；你太客氣了。
great〔gret〕*adj.* 很棒的

14. (**B**) How did you like the movie?

A. I enjoy movies very much.

B. It was so-so.

C. I'd love to.

* ***How did you like~*** ?　你喜不喜歡～?
enjoy〔ɪn'dʒɔɪ〕*v.* 喜歡
so-so〔'so,so〕*adj.* 馬馬虎虎的；普通的
I'd love to. 我很樂意。

15. (**B**) What were you doing in the park?

A. Let's play basketball.

B. I was taking a walk.

C. I always do it there.

* ***take a walk*** 散步 (= *go for a walk*)

16. (**A**) What do you think of our new teacher?

A. I like him.

B. I think he is new, too.

C. I don't think we will have a new teacher this year.

* ***think of*** 認為

17. (**A**) What are you watching?

    A. The basketball game on Channel 4.

    B. The novel *Harry Potter*.

    C. The radio.

    * channel〔'tʃænḷ〕*n.* 頻道   novel〔'nɑvḷ〕*n.* 小說
      Harry Potter 哈利波特（書名）
      radio〔'redɪ,o〕*n.* 收音機

18. (**A**) Have a nice vacation!

    A. Same to you.

    B. I have one, thank you.

    C. No, I haven't.

    * *Have a nice vacation!* 祝你假期愉快！
      Same to you. 你也是。（用於回答對方的祝福）

19. (**C**) Is it raining?

    A. Yes, it will.

    B. No, not very many.

    C. Yes, a little.

20. (**B**) Who won the game?

    A. We played two games.

    B. It was a tie.

    C. I want to play.

    * win〔wɪn〕*v.* 贏（三態變化為：win-won-won）
      game〔gem〕*n.* 比賽   play〔ple〕*v.* 打（球）
      tie〔taɪ〕*n.* 平手

第三部份

21. (**C**)　W：What are you reading?

　　　　　M：It's a textbook — Chinese history.

　　　　　W：Do you have a test tomorrow?

　　　　　M：No, I have to write a report.

　　　　　Question：What is the boy reading?

　　　　　A. A test.

　　　　　B. A report.

　　　　　C. A history book.

　　　　　* textbook (ˈtɛkst,buk) *n.* 教科書

　　　　　　history (ˈhɪstrɪ) *n.* 歷史

　　　　　　report (rɪˈport) *n.* 報告

22. (**B**)　W：It's so hot!

　　　　　M：I'm dying for a cold drink.

　　　　　W：Me, too.

　　　　　M：Look.　There's a Seven-Eleven over there.

　　　　　Question：How do they feel?

　　　　　A. Hungry.

　　　　　B. Thirsty.

　　　　　C. Sick.

　　　　　* so〔so 〕*adv.* 非常（ = *very*）

　　　　　　be dying for *sth.* 很渴望某物

　　　　　　drink〔drɪŋk 〕*n.* 飲料

　　　　　　thirsty (ˈθɝstɪ) *adj.* 口渴的

23. (**B**) M: Which team is your favorite?

W: I'm a Tigers fan. How about you?

M: Oh, I don't like any particular team. I just like to see a good game.

Question: What does the boy mean?

A. He doesn't like any team at all.

B. He likes every team the same amount.

C. He is a Tigers fan.

* team〔tim〕 *n.* 隊伍
  favorite〔'fevərɪt〕 *n.* 最喜愛的人或物
  fan〔fæn〕 *n.* (球) 迷　　***How about you?*** 那你呢？
  particular〔pə'tɪkjələ〕 *adj.* 特定的
  mean〔min〕 *v.* 意思是　　***not…at all*** 一點也不
  amount〔ə'maʊnt〕 *n.* 數量

24. (**A**) W: How old is your sister?

M: She's seven.

W: Has she started school?

M: Yes, she started this year.

Question: In which grade is the boy's sister?

A. The first grade of elementary school.

B. Seventh grade.

C. The first grade of senior high school.

* ***start school*** 開始上學 (= *begin school*)
  grade〔gred〕 *n.* 年級
  elementary〔͵ɛlə'mɛntərɪ〕 *adj.* 基本的；初級的
  elementary school 小學
  senior〔'sinjə〕 *adj.* 年長的；資深的
  senior high school 高中

25. (**A**) W: Congratulations! I heard you passed the exam.

M: Thank you. It was such a surprise.

W: Why should you be surprised? You studied hard for it.

Question: What does the girl think?

A. The boy deserved to pass the exam because he worked hard.

B. It is surprising that the boy passed the exam.

C. The boy should have studied harder for the exam.

* congratulations〔kən͵grætʃə'leʃənz〕 *n. pl.* 恭禧
  hear〔hɪr〕*v.* 聽說　　pass〔pæs〕*v.* 通過
  exam〔ɪg'zæm〕*n.* 考試　　surprise〔sə'praɪz〕*n.* 驚喜
  surprised〔sə'praɪzd〕*adj.* 驚訝的
  hard〔hɑrd〕*adv.* 認眞地；努力地
  deserve〔dɪ'zɝv〕*v.* 應得
  surprising〔sə'praɪzɪŋ〕*adj.* 令人驚訝的

26. (**B**) M: Excuse me, do you have change for 100 dollars?

W: I think so. Let me look.

M: Thanks. I need to take a bus.

W: Yes, here you are.

Question: What did the woman give to the man?

A. A bus ticket.　　　B. 100 dollars in change.

C. Fifteen dollars.

* change〔tʃendʒ〕*n.* 零錢
  Here you are. 拿去吧。(= *Here it is.* = *Here you go.*)
  100 dollars in change 100 元零錢

27. (**B**) M：Hey, turn to Channel four.

W：But I'm watching this.

M：You can watch cartoons anytime. My favorite program is starting now.

W：No way. I was here first.

M：Mom!

Question：What are they arguing about?

A. What time the program will start.

B. What to watch on television.

C. Where their mother is.

* ***turn to*** 轉到（電視頻道）　　cartoon〔kɑrˈtun〕 *n.* 卡通
anytime〔ˈɛnɪˌtaɪm〕 *adv.* 在任何時候
favorite〔ˈfevərɪt〕 *adj.* 最喜愛的
program〔ˈprogræm〕 *n.* 節目　　start〔stɑrt〕 *v.* 開始
No way. 不行。　　argue〔ˈɑrgju〕 *v.* 爭論 < *about* >

28. (**A**) W：That's a nice jacket.

M：Thanks.

W：Was it expensive?

M：No, it was on sale.

Question：What does the man mean?

A. He bought the jacket at a low price.

B. He wants to sell his jacket.

C. He would rather have an expensive jacket.

* jacket〔ˈdʒækɪt〕 *n.* 夾克
expensive〔ɪkˈspɛnsɪv〕 *adj.* 昂貴的　　***on sale*** 特價
at a low price 以低價　　***would rather*** 寧願

29. (**A**) W: Hello.

M: Is Monica there?

W: There is no one here by that name.

M: Oh, I'm sorry.

Question: What did the man do?

A. He called the wrong number.

B. He talked to Monica.

C. He lied to Monica.

* *There is no one here by that name.*
這裡沒有人叫那個名字。

call the wrong number 打錯電話號碼   lie〔laɪ〕*v.* 說謊

30. (**C**) W: Do you have any money?

M: No, I spent my pocket money already.

W: Already? But you got it only a couple of days ago.

M: Yeah. But I spent those two days playing on-line
games at the Internet café.

Question: What happened to the boy's money?

A. He lost it.

B. He spent it all on drinking coffee.

C. He used it to play on-line games.

* pocket〔'pakɪt〕*n.* 口袋   *pocket money* 零用錢
already〔ɔl'rɛdɪ〕*adv.* 已經
a couple of 幾個 (= *several*)
on-line〔'an'laɪn〕*adj.* 線上的；網路上的
Internet café 網咖   lose〔luz〕*v.* 遺失

二、閱讀能力測驗

第一部份：詞彙和結構

1. (**A**) Betty wants to be an <u>artist</u> because drawing is her passion.

貝蒂想成為一位<u>畫家</u>，因為她熱愛繪畫。

    (A) *artist* (ˊɑrtɪst) *n.* 藝術家；畫家（= *painter* ）

    (B) scientist (ˊsaɪəntɪst) *n.* 科學家

    (C) pianist (pɪˊænɪst) *n.* 鋼琴家

    (D) guitarist (gɪˊtɑrɪst) *n.* 吉他演奏家

  * drawing (ˊdrɔ·ɪŋ) *n.* 畫圖
   passion (ˊpæʃən) *n.* 熱愛；愛好

2. (**B**) All the guests thought the wedding was important, so they were all dressed in <u>formal</u> clothes.

所有來賓都認為婚禮很重要，所以他們全都穿著<u>正式的</u>服裝。

    (A) fluent (ˊfluənt) *adj.* 流利的

    (B) *formal* (ˊfɔrml) *adj.* 正式的

    (C) funny (ˊfʌnɪ) *adj.* 好笑的；有趣的

    (D) flat (flæt) *adj.* 平坦的

  * guest (gɛst) *n.* 客人；來賓   wedding (ˊwɛdɪŋ) *n.* 婚禮
   important (ɪmˊpɔrtn̩t) *adj.* 重要的
   be dressed in 穿著~

3. (**D**) Brenda didn't take the computer class because she couldn't <u>make</u> up her mind.

布蘭達沒有修電腦課，是因為她沒辦法<u>下定</u>決心。

   make up one's mind 下定決心

  * *take a class* 上課   computer (kəmˊpjutɚ) *n.* 電腦

4. (**D**) My <u>guess</u> is that he didn't come because his parents wouldn't let him. I'm not sure.

我<u>猜</u>他沒來，是因為他父母不讓他來。我不是很確定。

(A) plan〔plæn〕*n.* 計畫
(B) truth〔truθ〕*n.* 真相；事實
(C) knowledge〔'nɑlɪdʒ〕*n.* 知識
(D) *guess*〔gɛs〕*n.* 猜測

* let〔lɛt〕*v.* 讓（三態同形）　　sure〔ʃur〕*adj.* 確定的

5. (**B**) To <u>celebrate</u> my father's birthday, we are going to the mountains for a two-day vacation.

為了<u>慶祝</u>我父親的生日，我們要上山度假兩天。

(A) treat〔trit〕*v.* 對待；治療
(B) *celebrate*〔'sɛlə,bret〕*v.* 慶祝
(C) collect〔kə'lɛkt〕*v.* 收集
(D) allow〔ə'lau〕*v.* 允許

* mountain〔'mauntṇ〕*n.* 山
vacation〔ve'keʃən〕*n.* 假期

6. (**C**) <u>Can</u> you take a modern history class next semester?

你下學期<u>能夠</u>修現代歷史的課嗎？

依句意為未來式，且 take 為原形動詞，故空格填助動詞 *Can*，選 (C)。而 (A) did 須搭配表過去的時間副詞，與表未來的 next semester 不合，(B) have 用於完成式「have ＋過去分詞」的形式，(D) are 用於未來式「are going to」的形式，故用法皆不合。

* modern〔'mɑdən〕*adj.* 現代的
semester〔sə'mɛstə〕*n.* 學期

7. (**C**) I'm afraid <u>of</u> our neighbor's big dog.
我很<u>怕</u>我們鄰居養的那隻大狗。

be afraid of + **N.** 害怕

* neighbor〔'nebɚ〕 *n.* 鄰居

8. (**C**) Chinese New Year is coming, and all the people are
busy <u>cleaning</u> their houses.
農曆新年快到了，所有的人都忙著<u>打掃</u>家裡。

be busy + **V-ing** 忙於

* **Chinese New Year** 農曆新年   clean〔klin〕*v.* 打掃

9. (**A**) Go two blocks, <u>and</u> you'll see the bookstore.
走兩個街區，你<u>就會</u>看到書店。

祈使句, and + S. + V.（and 表「就會」）
祈使句, or + S. + V.（or 表「否則」）

本句也可說成：If you go two blocks, you'll see the
bookstore.

* block〔blɑk〕*n.* 街區   bookstore〔'bʊk,stor〕*n.* 書店

10. (**B**) Leo has quit smoking. He doesn't smoke <u>anymore</u>.
李奧已經戒煙。他<u>不再</u>抽煙了。

not…anymore 不再…

而 (A) again〔ə'gɛn〕 *adv.* 再一次，(C) anywhere
〔'ɛnɪ,hwɛr〕*adv.* 任何地方，(D) anyway〔'ɛnɪ,we〕*adv.*
無論如何，皆不合句意。

* quit〔kwɪt〕*v.* 戒除（三態同形）
smoke〔smok〕*v.* 抽煙   **quit smoking** 戒煙

11. (**C**) Last night, it took me almost three hours <u>to prepare</u> for the science test.

　　　昨晚，<u>準備</u>自然科小考花了我將近三個小時的時間。

　　　　take 表「花費 (時間)」的用法：
　　　　「It 或事物＋take＋人＋時間＋to V.」

　　* almost (ˈɔlˌmost) *adv.* 幾乎
　　　prepare (prɪˈpɛr) *v.* 準備 <*for*>
　　　science (ˈsaɪəns) *n.* 科學

12. (**D**) Two cute pandas came to Taiwan last September.

　　　去年九月，有兩隻可愛的貓熊來台。

　　　　last 開頭的時間副詞，不須搭配介系詞，故選 (D)。

　　* cute (kjut) *adj.* 可愛的　　panda (ˈpændə) *n.* 貓熊

13. (**C**) We have a cat <u>whose</u> color is black and white.

　　　我們有一隻顏色黑白相間的貓。

　　　　關係代名詞的所有格用 ***whose***，引導形容詞子句，修飾先
　　　行詞 cat。而 (A) who，(B) which，(D) that 雖是關係代
　　　名詞，但在其引導的形容詞子句中須做主詞或受詞，故用
　　　法不合。

　　* color (ˈkʌlə) *n.* 顏色　　***black and white*** 黑白的

14. (**B**) My sister wants a motorcycle, but she has no money to buy <u>one</u>.　我姊姊想要一台機車，但是她沒有錢買。

　　　　one 代替先前提到的名詞 a motorcycle，以避免重複。
　　　而 (A) the one，(C) it，(D) the other「另一個」，均有
　　　特定的意味，故用法皆不合。

　　* motorcycle (ˈmotəˌsaɪkḷ) *n.* 機車

15. (**C**) English is <u>so interesting</u> to me that I take every
opportunity to practice it.

英文對我而言<u>非常有趣</u>，所以我會把握每次練習的機會。

> ***so…that~*** 如此…以致於~

> interest「使感興趣」有兩個形容詞：

>> interesting 有趣的（修飾事物或人）
>> interested 有興趣的（修飾人）

> * take〔tek〕v. 利用　opportunity〔,ɑpɚˈtjunətɪ〕n. 機會
> practice〔ˈpræktɪs〕v. 練習

第二部份：段落填空

Questions 16-20

Billy had a terrible day today. First, he <u>was woken</u> up by a
16
strange call <u>at</u> three o'clock this morning. When he was going
17
to pick up the receiver, the phone stopped <u>ringing</u>. Then, he
18
overslept and <u>missed</u> the school bus, so he was thirty minutes late
19
for school. His teacher was very angry. What was <u>worse</u>, when
20
he got home this afternoon, he couldn't open the door because he
had left his keys in the classroom.

比利今天非常倒楣。首先，他今天早上凌晨三點就被一通奇怪的電
話吵醒。當他要拿起話筒時，電話鈴聲就停了。然後，他就睡過頭而沒
趕上校車，所以他到學校時，已經遲到三十分鐘。他的老師非常生氣。
更糟的是，他今天下午回家後，無法開門，因爲他把鑰匙留在敎室裡。

terrible〔'tɛrəbḷ〕*adj.* 糟糕的　　strange〔strendʒ〕*adj.* 奇怪的
pick up 拿起　　receiver〔rɪ'sivɚ〕*n.* 電話聽筒
oversleep〔'ovɚ'slip〕*v.* 睡過頭（三態變化爲：oversleep-
　　overslept-overslept）　　***school bus*** 校車
late〔let〕*adj.* 遲到的　　angry〔'æŋgrɪ〕*adj.* 生氣的
leave〔liv〕*v.* 遺留　　key〔ki〕*n.* 鑰匙

16.(**A**)　依句意，比利被奇怪的電話吵醒，用被動語態，即「be 動詞
　　　　＋過去分詞」的形式，又整篇敘述爲過去式，故選 (A) ***was***
　　　　woken。
　　　　wake〔wek〕*v.* 叫醒（三態變化爲：wake-woke-woken）

17.(**A**)　「在」凌晨三點鐘的時候，用介系詞 ***at***，選 (A)。

18.(**C**)　$\begin{cases} \text{stop} + \text{V-ing} \ \ 停止做～ \\ \text{stop} + \text{to V.} \ \ 停下來，去做～ \end{cases}$
　　　　按照句意，電話鈴聲停了，故選 (C) ***ringing***。
　　　　ring〔rɪŋ〕*v.* （鈴）響

19.(**D**)　(A) leave〔liv〕*v.* 離開　　(B) lose〔luz〕*v.* 失去
　　　　(C) catch〔kætʃ〕*v.* 趕上　　(D) ***miss***〔mɪs〕*v.* 錯過

20.(**A**)　***what is worse*** 更糟的是

Questions 21-25

Do you know what to do in an earthquake? When there is an earthquake, many things can fall down on you. So if you are inside, find a <u>safe</u> place such as under a table or in a doorway. If
　　　　　　　　　21
you are <u>outside</u>, go to an open area and <u>cover</u> your head. If you
　　　　　22　　　　　　　　　　　　　　23
are driving a car, stop the car at the side of the road and <u>wait</u>.
　　　　　　　　　　　　　　　　　　　　　　　　24
Stay in your safe place until the shaking stops. You cannot stop an earthquake, but you can be <u>ready</u> for one.
　　　　　　　　　　　　　　　　25

你知道地震時該怎麼辦嗎？地震發生的時候，可能會有很多東西掉到你身上。所以如果你是在室內，就要找個安全的地方，例如桌子下面或門口。如果你在室外，就找個空曠的地方，然後蓋住頭部。如果你正在開車，把車停在路邊等一下。待在安全的地方，直到震動停止。你無法阻止地震，但是你可以為地震做好準備。

earthquake (ˈɝθˌkwek) n. 地震　　***fall down*** 倒下；落下
inside (ˈɪnˈsaɪd) adv. 在室內　　***such as*** 像是 (= *like*)
doorway (ˈdorˌwe) n. 門口　　open (ˈopən) adj. 空曠的
area (ˈɛrɪə) n. 地區　　head (hɛd) n. 頭
drive (draɪv) v. 開車　　side (saɪd) n. 一側；一邊
photo (ˈfoto) n. 照片　　***in front of*** 在…前面
stay (ste) v. 停留　　safe (sef) adj. 安全的
until (ənˈtɪl) conj. 直到　　shaking (ˈʃekɪŋ) n. 搖動；震動

21. (**C**)　(A) quiet〔'kwaɪət〕*adj.* 安靜的

　　　　　(B) noisy〔'nɔɪzɪ〕*adj.* 吵鬧的

　　　　　(C) ***safe***〔sef〕*adj.* 安全的

　　　　　(D) dangerous〔'dendʒərəs〕*adj.* 危險的

22. (**A**)　依句意，前面先講到在室內的防震須知，後面再提到「在室
　　　　　外」的防震須知，故選 (A) ***outside*** (= *outdoors*)。

23. (**A**)　and 為對等連接詞，前後連接文法地位相等的單字、片語或子
　　　　　句，go 為原形動詞，故空格須填 (A) ***cover***〔'kʌvə〕遮蓋，
　　　　　形成祈使句。

24. (**D**)　(A) walk〔wɔk〕*v.* 走路

　　　　　(B) run〔rʌn〕*v.* 跑

　　　　　(C) jump〔dʒʌmp〕*v.* 跳

　　　　　(D) ***wait***〔wet〕*v.* 等待

25. (**B**)　(A) nervous〔'nɝvəs〕*adj.* 緊張的

　　　　　(B) ***ready***〔'rɛdɪ〕*adj.* 準備好的 < *for* >

　　　　　(C) surprised〔sə'praɪzd〕*adj.* 驚訝的

　　　　　(D) impressed〔ɪm'prɛst〕*adj.* 印象深刻的

第三部份：閱讀理解

Questions 26-28

書園
隆重開幕

「書園」終於來台灣了！別錯過我們下星期六開始的開幕慶祝活動！為期兩個禮拜，你將享有六到八折的優惠，購買你喜歡的書。我們有全國最多種類的書籍可供挑選，不論是小說、戲劇、詩、真人真事、雜誌等，應有盡有。

🎁 若是我們的第一千名顧客，將贏得大禮。

garden〔'gardn〕n. 花園　　grand〔grænd〕adj. 盛大的
opening〔'opənɪŋ〕n. 開幕　　finally〔'faɪnl̩ɪ〕adv. 最後；終於
arrive〔ə'raɪv〕v. 到達　　miss〔mɪs〕v. 錯過
celebration〔͵sɛlə'breʃən〕n. 慶祝（活動）
savings〔'sevɪŋz〕n. pl. 省下的錢
percent〔pə'sɛnt〕n. 百分比
selection〔sə'lɛkʃən〕n. 精選品
island〔'aɪlənd〕n. 島（在此指「台灣全省」）
fiction〔'fɪkʃən〕n. 小說　　drama〔'dramə〕n. 戲劇
poetry〔'poɪtrɪ〕n. 詩（總稱）
real-life〔'rɪəl͵laɪf〕adj. 真實的；現實的
magazine〔͵mægə'zin〕n. 雜誌
customer〔'kʌstəmɚ〕n. 顧客
present〔'prɛznt〕n. 禮物（= gift〔gɪft〕）

26. (**D**) 書園在慶祝什麼？

　　(A) 即將結束營業。

　　(B) 慶祝三十週年。

　　(C) 全球第一千家分店即將開幕。

　　(D) 台灣第一家分店即將開幕。

　　* close〔kloz〕v. 關閉；結束　　***in the world*** 在全世界

27. (**B**) 特賣將持續多久？

　　(A) 一個週末。

　　(B) 十四天。

　　(C) 一個禮拜。

　　(D) 一個月。

　　* sale〔sel〕n. 特賣　　last〔læst〕v. 持續
　　weekend〔'wik'ɛnd〕n. 週末

28. (**A**) 根據這則廣告，特價期間，書園沒有保證要做什麼？

　　(A) 書籍免費配送。

　　(B) 提供許多不同種類的書。

　　(C) 降低價錢。

　　(D) 送禮給第一千位顧客。

　　* ***according to*** 根據
　　advertisement〔͵ædvɚ'taɪzmənt〕n. 廣告
　　promise〔'pramɪs〕v. 保證
　　during〔'djʊrɪŋ〕prep. 在…期間
　　deliver〔dɪ'lɪvɚ〕v. 運送；遞送
　　free〔fri〕adv. 免費地　　offer〔'ɔfɚ〕v. 提供
　　different〔'dɪfrənt〕adj. 不同的　　kind〔kaɪnd〕n. 種類
　　lower〔'loɚ〕v. 降低　　price〔praɪs〕n. 價錢

Questions 29-30

這是一本書中六課的目錄。仔細閱讀後，回答問題。

第一課	我愛電子郵件 ✗✗✗✗✗✗✗✗✗✗✗✗	1
第二課	健康飲食 ✗✗✗✗✗✗✗✗✗✗✗✗✗✗	16
第三課	輕鬆減肥 ✗✗✗✗✗✗✗✗✗✗✗✗✗✗	28
第四課	用雙手說話 ✗✗✗✗✗✗✗✗✗✗✗✗	40
第五課	未來世界 ✗✗✗✗✗✗✗✗✗✗✗✗✗✗	58
第六課	信不信由你 ✗✗✗✗✗✗✗✗✗✗✗✗	70

contents〔ˈkɑntɛnts〕*n. pl.* (書刊等的) 目錄
carefully〔ˈkɛrfəlɪ〕*adv.* 仔細地
e-mail〔ˈiˌmel〕*n.* 電子郵件　　healthy〔ˈhɛlθɪ〕*adj.* 健康的
diet〔ˈdaɪət〕*n.* 飲食　　***lose weight*** 減肥
easily〔ˈizɪlɪ〕*adv.* 容易地；輕鬆地
future〔ˈfjutʃɚ〕*adj.* 未來的　　believe〔bɪˈliv〕*v.* 相信
believe it or not 信不信由你

29. (**D**) 無法說話的人，可以靠動手指，來告訴其他人他們想說什麼。
約瑟夫想知道更多有關手語的事。哪一課對他有幫助？

(A) 第一課。　　　　　　　(B) 第二課。
(C) 第三課。　　　　　　　(D) 第四課。

* move〔muv〕*v.* 移動　　finger〔ˈfɪŋgɚ〕*n.* 手指
useful〔ˈjusfəl〕*adj.* 有用的

30. (**B**) 下列敘述何者不正確？

(A) 第一課是關於電腦。

(B) 第五課比第一課長。

(C) 最後一課或許有奇怪的故事。

(D) 想減肥的人應該看第二課及第三課。

* following〔ˋfɑləwɪŋ〕 *adj.* 下列的

true〔tru〕 *adj.* 真實的；正確的

strange〔strendʒ〕 *adj.* 奇怪的

last〔læst〕 *adj.* 最後的　　 ***go on a diet*** 節食；減肥

Question 31

31. (**B**) 這個告示牌是什麼意思？

(A) 禁止停車。

(B) 繫上安全帶。

(C) 禁止進入。

(D) 出口。

* sign〔saɪn〕 *n.* 告示牌　　 mean〔min〕 *v.* 意思是

park〔pɑrk〕 *v.* 停車　　 fasten〔ˋfæsn̩〕 *v.* 繫上

seat belt 安全帶　　 enter〔ˋɛntɚ〕 *v.* 進入

exit〔ˋɛgzɪt, -sɪt〕 *n.* 出口

Questions 32-33

March 1, 2003

Dear son,

How are you? It's just one month since I came to Canada. I'm learning English after work because I need to talk to people around me in English.

Last night, my English teacher, Mr. Smith, said to me, "You look tired. How come, Mr. Liu?" I said, "How…come…? Well, I…I…I come here by subway." The teacher said, "I know you come here by subway, but how come you are tired?" I didn't understand him well and didn't say anything. Then he smiled and said, "Well, I am asking why you are tired."

I know both "how" and "come," but I didn't understand "How come?" It was really new to me. Have you learned it at school? English is interesting, isn't it? Every day I'm learning new things in this way. I have had a lot of wonderful experience. How about you?

I hope to hear from you soon.

With love,
Dad

2003 年 3 月 1 日

親愛的兒子：

　　你好嗎？我來加拿大才一個月而已。我現在下班後去學英文，因為我必須跟周遭的人用英語交談。

　　昨天晚上，我的英文老師史密斯先生對我說：「你看起來很累。劉先生，為什麼？」我說：「如何…來…？嗯，我…我…我坐地下鐵來的。」老師說：「我知道你坐地鐵來的，可是你怎麼會這麼累呢？」我不太清楚他的意思，所以我就沒說話了。然後他微笑說著：「嗯，我是問你為何如此疲倦。」

　　我知道「如何」跟「來」的意思，可是我不知道什麼是「為什麼？」這對我而言真的是新的東西。你在學校有學過嗎？英文真有趣，不是嗎？每天我都用這種方式學習新事物。我有很多很棒的經驗。那你呢？

　　希望能很快收到你的回信。

愛你的，
父親

son〔sʌn〕n. 兒子   since〔sɪns〕conj. 自從
Canada〔'kænədə〕n. 加拿大   **after work** 下班後
around〔ə'raʊnd〕prep. 在…周圍
in 表「用～（語言）」。   **how come** 爲什麼
subway〔'sʌb,we〕n. 地下鐵（＝Metro〔'mɛtro〕）
understand〔ˌʌndɚ'stænd〕v. 了解   smile〔smaɪl〕v. 微笑
new〔nju〕adj. 陌生的＜to＞   **in this way** 用這種方式
a lot of 許多的   wonderful〔'wʌndɚfəl〕adj. 很棒的
experience〔ɪk'spɪrɪəns〕n. 經驗
hear from sb. 得知某人的消息；收到某人的來信
dad〔dæd〕n. 爸爸

32.（**C**）下列敘述何者正確？

(A) 這是一封女兒寫給父親的信。

(B) 劉先生很累，因爲在地鐵上班。

(C) 劉先生於二月初到加拿大。

(D) 劉先生在上完英文課後工作。

* letter〔'lɛtɚ〕n. 信
 daughter〔'dɔtɚ〕n. 女兒
 beginning〔bɪ'gɪnɪŋ〕n. 起初；開始

33.（**B**）如果史密斯先生問劉先生："How come you are late?"，
這是什麼意思？

(A) 你是如何晚來的？

(B) 你爲什麼遲到？

(C) 你爲何不遲到？

(D) 你如何遲到的？

Questions 34-35

I had a funny dream last night. I dreamed that I became
Superman. I was smart and strong. I had the best grades in my
class. I was good at playing basketball, baseball and volleyball.
At the same time, I was the captain of all three school teams.

我昨晚做了一個好笑的夢。我夢見我變成超人。我既聰明又強壯。
我在班上成績最好。我擅長打籃球、棒球和排球。同時我還是這三個校
隊的隊長。

funny〔'fʌnɪ〕adj. 好笑的　　dream〔drim〕n. 夢　v. 夢見
Superman〔'supə,mæn〕n. 超人　　smart〔smɑrt〕adj. 聰明的
strong〔strɔŋ〕adj. 強壯的　　grade〔gred〕n. 分數；成績
be good at 擅長　　play〔ple〕v. 打（球）
volleyball〔'vɑlɪ,bɔl〕n. 排球　　**at the same time** 同時
captain〔'kæptɪn〕n.（運動團隊的）隊長　　**school team** 校隊

After school, I wore Superman clothing and helped people in
need. I helped an old lady cross the road and a little girl take her
kite down from a tree. I also helped the police catch bad people.
I did so many good things that the President invited me to have
dinner. But I didn't accept his invitation because I had to study
for my final exam. What a strange ending my dream had!

放學後，我穿上超人裝，然後幫助窮困的人。我幫忙一位老太太過
馬路，還幫一位小女孩把她的風箏從樹上拿下來。我也幫警方抓壞人。
我做了這麼多好事，所以總統邀請我共進晚餐。但是我沒有接受他的邀
請，因爲我必須準備期末考。這場夢的結局，多麼奇怪啊！

after school 放學後

wear〔wɛr〕v. 穿（三態變化爲：wear-wore-worn）

clothing〔'kloðɪŋ〕n. 衣服　*in need* 在窮困中的

cross〔krɔs〕v. 越過　*take down* （從高處）取下

kite〔kaɪt〕n. 風箏　*the police* 警方

catch〔kætʃ〕v. 逮捕；抓到　president〔'prɛzədnt〕n. 總統

invite〔ɪn'vaɪt〕v. 邀請　have〔hæv〕v. 吃

accept〔ək'sɛpt〕v. 接受　invitation〔,ɪnvə'teʃən〕n. 邀請

final exam 期末考　ending〔'ɛndɪŋ〕n. （故事等的）結局

34. (**A**) 作者昨天晚上夢見什麼？

(A) 他是超人。

(B) 他偶然遇見超人。

(C) 超人幫助他。

(D) 超人教他在籃球比賽中，如何投籃投得準。

* writer〔'raɪtə〕n. 作者　*bump into* 偶然遇到

　shot〔ʃɑt〕n. 投籃

35. (**B**) 作者在夢中，放學後做什麼？

(A) 在公車上，他讓位給一名警察。

(B) 他幫一個小女孩把她的風箏從樹上拿下來。

(C) 他和總統共進晚餐。

(D) 他忘記他的夢最後發生了什麼事情。

* *give one's seat to* 讓位給～

　policeman〔pə'lismən〕n. 警察

　forget〔fə'gɛt〕v. 忘記　happen〔'hæpən〕v. 發生

　end〔ɛnd〕n. 最後部分　*at the end of* 在～的最後

三、寫作能力測驗

第一部份：單句寫作

第 1～5 題：句子改寫

1. She wrote this famous novel.

   This famous novel ＿＿＿＿＿＿＿＿＿＿＿＿＿＿ her.

   > 重點結構：被動語態字序
   >
   > 解　答：This famous novel was written by her.
   >
   > 句型分析：主詞＋be 動詞＋過去分詞＋by＋受詞
   >
   > 說　明：被動語態的形式是「be 動詞＋過去分詞」，故動詞
   > wrote 須改為 was written。
   >
   > * famous (ˈfeməs) adj. 有名的　　novel (ˈnɑvḷ) n. 小說

2. Listening to popular music is fun.

   It's ＿＿＿＿＿＿＿＿＿＿＿＿＿＿＿＿＿＿＿＿＿.

   > 重點結構：以 It 為虛主詞引導的句子
   >
   > 解　答：It's fun to listen to popular music.
   >
   > 句型分析：It's ＋形容詞＋ to V.
   >
   > 說　明：虛主詞 It 代替不定詞片語，不定詞片語則擺在句
   > 尾，故 Listening to popular music 改為 to listen
   > to popular music。
   >
   > * *listen to* 聽　　popular (ˈpɑpjələ) adj. 流行的
   > fun (fʌn) adj. 有趣的

3. When will the next bus come?
   I'd like to know when _____.

   重點結構：間接問句做名詞子句

   解　答：I'd like to know when the next bus will come.

   句型分析：I'd like to know + when + 主詞 + 動詞

   説　明：在 wh-問句前加 I'd like to know，形成名詞子句
   　　　　（間接問句），即「疑問詞 + 主詞 + 動詞」的形
   　　　　式，把 will come 放在最後面，並把問號改成句點。

4. Nicolas went home after school.
   Where _____ after school?

   重點結構：過去式的 wh-問句

   解　答：Where did Nicolas go after school?

   句型分析：Where + did + 主詞 + 原形動詞？

   説　明：這一題應將過去式直述句改為 wh-問句，除了要加助
   　　　　動詞 did，還要記得助動詞後面的動詞，須用原形動
   　　　　詞，因此 went 要改成 go。

5. My friend gave me a stuffed doll.
   My friend _____ me.

   重點結構：give 的用法

   解　答：My friend gave a stuffed doll to me.

   句型分析：give + 直接受詞（物）+ to + 間接受詞（人）

   説　明：「把東西給某人」有兩種寫法：「give + sb. + sth.」
   　　　　或「give + sth. + to + sb.」，這題要改成第二種
   　　　　用法，先寫物（a stuffed doll），再寫人（me）。

   * stuffed〔stʌft〕adj. 填充（玩具）的　　doll〔dɑl〕n. 洋娃娃

第 6～10 題：句子合併

6. Don't drink too much coffee.

You will not fall asleep easily.

Don't drink too much coffee, _____.

重點結構：祈使句表達條件句的用法

解　答：Don't drink too much coffee, or you will not fall asleep easily.

句型分析：原形動詞，or + 主詞 + 動詞

説　明：這題的意思是說「不要喝太多咖啡，不然你會不容易入睡」，連接詞 or 表「否則」。這題可改寫為：*If* you drink too much coffee, you will not fall asleep easily.

＊ coffee ('kɔfɪ) *n.* 咖啡　　***fall asleep*** 睡著

7. We had a music class this morning.

We had a PE class this morning.

We had both a music _____ this morning.

重點結構：both A and B 的用法

解　答：We had both a music (class) and a PE class this morning.

句型分析：主詞 + 動詞 + both + 名詞 + and + 名詞

説　明：句意是「我們今天早上，不但有音樂課，還有體育課」，用「both…and～」合併兩個受詞，表「不但…而且～」。

＊ ***PE*** 體育 (＝ *physical education*)

8. The rain is very heavy.

Tammy cannot drive safely.

The rain is too heavy for Tammy _____.

重點結構：「too + 形容詞 + to V.」的用法

解　答：<u>The rain is too heavy for Tammy to drive safely.</u>

句型分析：主詞 + be 動詞 + too + 形容詞 + to V.

說　明：這題的意思是說「雨太大了，所以泰咪不能安全地駕駛」，用「too…to V.」合併兩句，表「太…以致於不～」。

* heavy〔ˈhɛvɪ〕adj. 大量的　　safely〔ˈseflɪ〕adv. 安全地

9. A cup of coffee costs 50 dollars.

A cup of tea costs 60 dollars.

A cup of tea is _____ than a cup of coffee.

重點結構：形容詞比較級的用法

解　答：<u>A cup of tea is more expensive than a cup of coffee.</u>

句型分析：主詞 + be 動詞 + 比較級形容詞 + than + 受詞

說　明：從 than 可看出這是「比較級」的句型，而一杯咖啡（50元）和一杯茶（60元）的價錢相較之下，茶比較貴，故用 more expensive，形成比較級。

10. Ron is very old.

He can drive a car.

Ron is old enough _____.

　　重點結構：「形容詞 + enough + to V.」的用法

　　　解　答：<u>Ron is old enough to drive a car.</u>

　　句型分析：主詞 + be 動詞 + 形容詞 + enough + to V.

　　　說　明：這題的意思是說「朗年紀夠大，可以開車了」，副
　　　　　　　詞 enough「足夠地」須置於要修飾的形容詞之後，
　　　　　　　「足以～」則以 enough 加不定詞表示。

第 11～15 題：重組

11. Caroline _____.

couldn't sleep / that / nervous / she / so / was

　　重點結構：「so + 形容詞 + that 子句」的用法

　　　解　答：<u>Caroline was so nervous that she couldn't sleep.</u>

　　句型分析：主詞 + be 動詞 + so + 形容詞 + that + 主詞 + 動詞

　　　說　明：這題的意思是說「凱洛琳太緊張了，所以睡不著」，
　　　　　　　合併兩句時，用「so…that～」，表「如此…以致
　　　　　　　於～」。

　＊ nervous〔ˋnɝvəs〕adj. 緊張的

12. Neither I _____.
    can / sister / my / nor / cook

　　重點結構：「neither…nor～」的用法

　　解　答：Neither I nor my sister can cook.

　　句型分析：Neither + A + nor + B + 助動詞 + 動詞

　　説　明：這題是說我不會說做菜，我姊姊也不會做菜，所以
　　　　　　兩個人都不會做菜，用「neither…nor～」來連接
　　　　　　兩個主詞，表「兩者皆不」。

　　* cook〔kʊk〕v. 煮飯；做菜

13. I asked Mother _____.
    at the station / she / pick me up / could / if

　　重點結構：由連接詞 if 引導的子句

　　解　答：I asked Mother if she could pick me up at the
　　　　　　station.

　　句型分析：I asked Mother + if + 主詞 + 動詞

　　説　明：I asked Mother 後面少受詞，現在 if（是否）引導
　　　　　　名詞子句，做 I asked Mother 的受詞，即名詞子句
　　　　　　「連接詞 + 主詞 + 動詞」的形式。

　　* pick sb. up　開車接某人

14. Jenny _____.

Nicolas / a pen / his birthday / sent / for

重點結構：send 的用法

解　答：<u>Jenny sent Nicolas a pen for his birthday.</u>

句型分析：send + 間接受詞（人）+ 直接受詞（物）

說　明：「寄東西給某人」有兩種寫法：「send + *sb.* + *sth.*」
或「send + *sth.* + to + *sb.*」，題目中沒有介系詞
to，所以要採用第一種寫法，先寫人（Nicolas），
再寫物（a pen），而 for 表「為了～（原因）」。

15. _____, please?

paper / you / me / another / Could / give

重點結構：Could 開頭問句的用法

解　答：<u>Could you give me another paper, please?</u>

句型分析：Could + 主詞 + 動詞？

說　明：本句是問「可以請你給我另外一張紙嗎？」即問句
的形式，先寫助動詞 Could，再寫主詞。

第二部份：段落寫作

題目： 昨天你和朋友坐捷運到動物園，看到你最喜歡的動物——企鵝
（penguins），請根據圖片內容寫一篇約 50 字的簡短描述。

Yesterday I went to the zoo with my friend. We took the
MRT. It was very fast. When we got there, there were many
people waiting in line. We bought our tickets and went inside.
We saw many animals in the zoo. I liked them all, ***but*** my
favorite animals were the penguins. I had a very good time
at the zoo yesterday.

zoo〔zu〕*n.* 動物園
MRT 大眾捷運系統（= *Mass Rapid Transit*）
wait in line 排隊等候　　ticket〔'tɪkɪt〕*n.* 門票
inside〔'ɪn'saɪd〕*adv.* 往裡面　　animal〔'ænəml̩〕*n.* 動物
penguin〔'pɛngwɪn〕*n.* 企鵝　　***have a good time*** 玩得愉快

附錄

全民英語能力分級檢定測驗簡介

「全民英語能力分級檢定測驗」（General English Proficiency Test），簡稱「全民英檢」（GEPT），旨在提供我國各階段英語學習者 公平、可靠、具效度之英語能力評量工具，測驗對象包括在校學生及一般社會人士，可做為學習成果檢定、教學改進及公民營機構甄選人才等之參考。

本測驗為標準參照測驗（criterion-referenced test），參考當前我國英語教育體制，制定分級標準，整套系統共分五級——初級（Elementary）、中級（Intermediate）、中高級（High-Intermediate）、高級（Advanced）、優級（Superior）。每級訂有明確能力標準（詳見表一綜合能力說明），報考者可依英語能力選擇適當級數報考，每級均包含聽、說、讀、寫四項完整的測驗，通過所報考級數的能力標準即可取得該級的合格證書。各級命題設計均參考目前各階段英語教育之課程大綱及相關教材之內容分析，期能符合國內各階段英語教育的需求、反應本土的生活經驗與特色。

「全民英語能力檢定分級測驗」各級綜合能力說明　　《表一》

級數	綜合能力	備註	
初級	通過初級測驗者具有基礎英語能力，能理解和使用淺易日常用語，英語能力相當於國中畢業者。	建議下列人員宜具有該級英語能力	一般行政助理、維修技術人員、百貨業、餐飲業、旅館業或觀光景點服務人員、計程車駕駛等。
中級	通過中級測驗者具有使用簡單英語進行日常生活溝通的能力，英語能力相當於高中職畢業者。		一般行政、業務、技術、銷售人員、護理人員、旅館、飯店接待人員、總機人員、警政人員、旅遊從業人員等。
中高級	通過中高級測驗者英語能力逐漸成熟，應用的領域擴大，雖有錯誤，但無礙溝通，英語能力相當於大學非英語主修系所畢業者。		商務、企劃人員、祕書、工程師、研究助理、空服人員、航空機師、航管人員、海關人員、導遊、外事警政人員、新聞從業人員、資訊管理人員等。

級數	綜　合　能　力		備　　　註
高級	通過高級測驗者英語流利順暢，僅有少許錯誤，應用能力擴及學術或專業領域，英語能力相當於國內大學英語主修系所或曾赴英語系國家大學或研究所進修並取得學位者。	建議下列人員宜具有該級英語能力	高級商務人員、協商談判人員、英語教學人員、研究人員、翻譯人員、外交人員、國際新聞從業人員等。
優級	通過優級測驗者的英語能力接近受過高等教育之母語人士，各種場合均能使用適當策略作最有效的溝通。		專業翻譯人員、國際新聞特派人員、外交官員、協商談判主談人員等。

初級英語能力測驗簡介

I. 通過初級檢定者的英語能力

聽	說	讀	寫
能聽懂簡易的英語句子、對話及故事。	能簡單地自我介紹並以簡易英語對答；能朗讀簡易文章。	能瞭解簡易英語對話、短文、故事及書信的內容；能看懂常用的標示。	能寫簡單的英語句子及段落。

II. 測 驗 內 容

測驗項目	初　試			複　試
	聽力測驗	閱讀能力測驗	寫作能力測驗	口說能力測驗
總題數	30	35	16	18
作答時間/分鐘	約 20	35	40	約 10
測驗內容	看圖辨義 問答 簡短對話	詞彙和結構 段落填空 閱讀理解	單句寫作 段落寫作	複誦 朗讀句子與短文 回答問題

　　聽力及閱讀能力測驗成績採標準計分方式，60分為平均數，滿分120分。寫作及口說能力測驗成績採整體式評分，使用級分制，分為0～5級分，再轉換成百分制。各項成績通過標準如下：

Ⅲ. 成績計算及通過標準

初　試	通過標準 / 滿分	複　試	通過標準 / 滿分
聽力測驗 閱讀能力測驗 寫作能力測驗	80 / 120 分 80 / 120 分 70 / 100 分	口說能力測驗	80 / 100 分

Ⅳ. 寫作能力測驗級分說明

第一部份：單句寫作級分說明

級　分	說　　　　明
2	正確無誤。
1	有誤，但重點結構正確。
0	錯誤過多、未答、等同未答。

第二部份：段落寫作級分說明

級　分	說　　　　明
5	正確表達題目之要求；文法、用字等幾乎無誤。
4	大致正確表達題目之要求；文法、用字等有誤，但不影響讀者之理解。
3	大致回答題目之要求，但未能完全達意；文法、用字等有誤，稍影響讀者之理解。
2	部份回答題目之要求，表達上有令人不解/誤解之處；文法、用字等皆有誤，讀者須耐心解讀。
1	僅回答1個問題或重點；文法、用字等錯誤過多，嚴重影響讀者之理解。
0	未答、等同未答。

各部份題型之題數、級分及總分計算公式：

分項測驗	測驗題型	各部份題數	每題級分	佔總分比重
第一部份：單句寫作	A. 句子改寫	5題	2分	50％
	B. 句子合併	5題	2分	
	C. 重組	5題	2分	
第二部份：段落寫作	看圖表寫作	1篇	5分	50％
總分計算公式	公式：{(第一部份得分/30) + (第二部份得分/5)}×50 例：第一部份各項得分 A－8分　　　　　　　　　　　B－10分　　　　　　　　　　　C－8分 8+10+8=26 三項加總第一部份得分 － 26分 第二部份得分 － 4分 依公式計算如下： {(26/30) + (4/5)}×50=83　該考生得分83分			

　　凡應考且合乎規定者一律發給成績單。初試及複試各項測驗成績通過者，發給合格證書，本測驗成績紀錄保存兩年。

　　初試通過者，可於一年內單獨報考複試，得重複報考。惟複試一旦通過，即不得再報考。

　　已通過本英檢測驗初級，一年內不得再報考同級數之測驗。違反本規定報考者，其應試資格將被取消，且不退費。

（以上資料取自「全民英檢學習網站」http://www.gept.org.tw）

⊖FPT®

全民英語能力分級檢定測驗合格證書
Certificate of General English Proficiency

姓　名：林銀姿
Name　LIN YIN-TZU
　　　　(#011102253)

身分證字號
Identification No.: F223910696

級　業：初級
Level：Elementary

測驗日期
Test Date：2001/05/26

證書編號
Serial No.: E000722

發證日期
Date of Issue：2001/06/21

茲證明右列應試者參加財團法人語言訓練測驗中心舉辦之全民英語能力分級檢定測驗已達右列級數合格標準。

This is to certify that the person whose name appears on the right has passed the indicated level of the General English Proficiency Test administered by the Language Training and Testing Center.

核發單位：　**LTTC** 財團法人語言訓練測驗中心
Issuer　　　The Language Training and Testing Center

陸　慶　來　Lu Chen-Lai
主任　陸慶來，Executive Director
Lu Chen-Lai, Executive Director

指導單位：中華民國教育部
Under the auspices of the Ministry of Education, R.O.C.

本頁無簽署本無效。Invalid without Authorized Signature

初級英語檢定模考班

　　21世紀是證照的時代，一般服務業，如行政助理、百貨業、餐飲業、旅館業、觀光景點服務人員及計程車駕駛等，均須通過此項測驗。

　　「初級英語檢定測驗」初試項目包含①聽力測驗－分為看圖辨義、問答、簡短對話三部分。②閱讀能力測驗－分為詞彙和結構、段落填空、閱讀理解三部分。③寫作能力測驗－包含單句寫作及段落寫作二部分。

- **招生目的**：協助同學通過「初級英語檢定測驗」。

- **招生對象**：任何人均可以參加。通過初級測驗者具有基礎英語能力，能理解和使用淺易日常用語。

- **上課時間**：每週日下午 2:00 ~ 5:00（共八週）

- **收費標準**：4800 元（劉毅英文家教班學生僅收 3800 元）

- **上課內容**：完全比照財團法人語言訓練中心所做「初級英語檢定測驗」初試標準。分為聽力測驗、閱讀能力測驗，及寫作能力測驗三部分。每次上課舉行 70 分鐘的模擬考，包含 30 題聽力測驗，35 題詞彙結構、段落填空、閱讀理解、及 15 題單句寫作、及一篇段落寫作。考完試後立即講解，馬上釐清所有問題。

劉毅英文家教班（國一、國二、國三、高一、高二、高三班）

班址：台北市重慶南路一段 10 號 7 F（火車站前‧日盛銀行樓上）
電話：(02) 2381-3148‧2331-8822　　網址：www.learnschool.com.tw

國一、國二英文家教班

I. **招生對象**：國一、國二同學

II. **教學目標**：協助國一、國二同學，在校月期考成績名列前茅。

III. **開課班級**：

國　　A　班	每週六上午 9：00 ～ 12：00
國　一　B　班	每週五晚上 6：30 ～ 9：30
國　二　A　班	每週六下午 2：00 ～ 5：00
國　二　B　班	每週日上午 9：00 ～ 12：00

IV. **獎學金制度**：

1. 蒐集各校月期考試題，及歷年來學校考古題，本班講義完全按照學校月考、期考測驗題型編排。

2. 學校段考，只要有一次英文科是班上前五名，**可得獎學金 *1000* 元。**

3. 每次來本班週考，考得好有獎，進步也有獎，各種獎勵很多。

4. 報名後，即開始背國中單字，優先口試通過者，**可得獎學金 *1000* 元。**

V. **授課內容**：

1. 蒐集各校月期考試題，及歷年來學校考古題，本班講義完全按照學校月考、期考測驗題型編排。

2. 每週上課前先考 50 分鐘週考，考後老師立即講解，馬上釐清同學錯誤的觀念。**當天考卷改完，立即發還。**

3. 每週檢討完週考考卷後，老師再將課本內容、重點仔細講解一遍，除了加強課外閱讀能力，亦可兼顧學校課程。**「學校月期考」**得高分的秘訣，就是：**週考➡上課檢討➡課文重點講解➡針對弱點加以加強➡月期考得高分。**

4. 國一、國二班，特別強調發音，在同學舌頭還沒有硬以前，和美籍老師用英文交談，經過本班訓練後，終身受益。

劉毅英文家教班（國一、國二、國三、高一、高二、高三班）

班址：台北市重慶南路一段 10 號 7F（消防隊斜對面）　　☎（02）2381-3148・2331-8822

劉毅英文國三基本學力測驗模考班

I. **招生對象：** 國中三年級同學

II. **教學目標：** 協助國三同學，順利通過「國中基本學力測驗」，和「各校第二階段甄選入學考試」。

III. **開課班級：**

英文 A 班	每週六下午 2：00～ 5：00	數 學 班	每週日下午 1：30～ 4：30
英文 B 班	每週六晚上 6：00～ 9：00	理 化 班	每週六晚上 6：00～ 9：00
英文 C 班	每週日上午 9：00～12：00	國 文 班	每週六上午 9：00～12：00

IV. **獎學金制度：**
　　1. 本班同學在學校班上，國二下學期或國三上學期總成績，只要有一次第一名者，可獲得獎學金*3000*元，第二名*1000*元，第三名*1000*元。

　　2. 學校模擬考試，只要有一次班上前五名，可得獎學金*1000*元。

　　3. 每次來本班考模擬考試，考得好有獎，進步也有獎，各種獎勵很多。

V. **授課內容：**

　　1. 本班獨創**模擬考制度**。
　　　根據92年「基本學力測驗」最新命題趨勢，蒐集命題委員參考資料，完全比照學力測驗題型編排。「基本學力測驗」得高分的祕訣，就是：**模擬考試➡上課檢討➡針對弱點加以加強**。

　　2. **本班掌握最新命題趨勢**：題型全爲單一選擇題、題材以多樣化及實用性爲原則。英文科加考書信、時刻表等題型；數學科則著重觀念題型，須建立基本觀念，融會貫通；理化科著重於實驗及原理運用。我們聘請知名高中學校老師（如建中、北一女、師大附中、中山、成功等），**完全按照基本學力測驗的題型命題**。

　　3. 每週上課前先考 50 分鐘模擬考，考後老師立即講解，馬上整清同學錯誤的觀念。**當天考卷改完，立即發還**。

龍門補門班・劉毅英文（國一、國二、國三、高一、高二、高三班）

班址：台北市重慶南路一段10號7F(捷運重慶南路出口處) ☎(02)2381-3148・2331-8822

劉毅英文家教班國三基本學力測驗模擬考比賽
成績優勝同學名單

※ 基本學力測驗滿分為 60 分。

姓名	學校	分數	姓名	學校	分數	姓名	學校	分數	姓名	學校	分數
徐子淳	中正國中	57	王大齊	中正國中	49	謝佩瑾	萬芳國中	45	施尹婷	北投國中	43
梁智景	方濟國中	57	詹舒涵	陽明國中	49	田雅汶	福和國中	45	游騏蔚	永和國中	42
林楷軒	仁愛國中	56	林韋廷	金華國中	49	蔡竣傑	康橋國小	45	許芳穎	明德國中	42
羅聖皓	南門國中	56	林俊甫	林口國中	49	楊平	金華國中	45	袁芷軒	金陵女中	42
郭鈞鰲	仁愛國中	56	周維新	靜心中學	49	陳沛穎	秀峰國中	45	駱柏蒼	三芝國中	42
洪誼齡	延平國中	55	莊維釗	景興國中	49	莊博宇	金華國中	45	胡庭毓	弘道國中	42
蒼奇勳	永吉國中	55	陳端翔	景興國中	49	陳詠清	薇閣中學	45	陳泓瑞	秀峰國中	42
林育如	金陵國中	55	許涵瑩	五峰國中	48	林祐安	重慶國中	45	洪嘉駿	長庚國中	42
廖桂箏	恆毅國中	55	蔡孟芸	師大附中	48	蔣尋安	中正國中	45	賴柏宏	新莊國中	42
林彥廷	師大附中	55	李玲	福利國中	48	施云婷	師大附中	44	涂盈孜	萬華國中	42
王玉婕	實踐國中	54	曹虰鑑	明德國中	48	余炎凌	三民國中	44	王維萱	延平國中	42
陳豈單	板橋國中	54	陳姝予	南渡國中	48	卓欣怡	金華國中	44	陳昱吟	龍山國中	42
顏悅涵	文山國中	54	范純融	和平國中	48	李宜瑾	蘭雅國中	44	卓文能	華興國中	42
鄧嘉薇	東山國中	54	洪子婷	明德國中	48	王鞸澄	師大附中	44	張家瑋	海山國中	42
黃郁喬	金華國中	54	沈容閔	銘傳國中	48	賴永翰	介壽國中	44	張之龍	芳和國中	42
何牧	復興國中	54	翁嘉伶	再興高中	48	潘采蝶	仁愛國中	44	林宜璇	仁愛國中	42
蔡昉晃	中山國中	54	陳瓊怡	天母國中	48	游淑惟	江翠國中	44	周傳傑	景美國中	42
江采蓮	永和國中	54	林佳錦	永樂國小	47	孫少傳	仁愛國中	44	林苑茹	增公國中	42
彭文彥	光仁國中	54	余敏嘉	民生國中	47	劉俊霆	金華國中	44	吳秀娟	仁愛國中	42
吳佩芝	蘭雅國中	54	施懿民	金陵女中	47	劉方瑀	敦化國中	44	黃敬恆	中正國中	42
姜庭歡	敦化國中	54	張維芯	萬芳國中	47	林姿吟	中正國中	44	周幸怡	士林國中	42
原琬婷	大安國中	53	林長青	金華國中	47	施竺雅	西湖國中	44	陳昭安	復興國中	41
張韶庭	景美國中	53	白芮寧	仁愛國中	47	熊妍惠	華興國中	44	陸致遠	民生國中	41
沈建宏	中山國中	53	陳怡雯	秀峰國中	47	林承翰	弘道國中	44	任書儀	聖心國中	41
施姵甫	萬華國中	53	王沛渝	敦化國中	47	李鎮亞	海山中學	44	黃皓	永和國中	41
張雯雯	蘭雅國中	53	林家安	東山國中	47	游子杰	福和國中	44	周浣盈	敦化國中	41
顏君恬	薇閣國中	53	陳思源	溪崑國中	47	蘇怡帆	南門國中	44	簡億如	石牌國中	41
鄭瑜萱	光仁國中	53	陳忻昀	醒吾中學	47	劉宗翰	金華國中	44	余心蓓	和平國中	41
高嘉良	江翠國中	52	許原浩	延平中學	46.29	廖珮吟	金華國中	44	盧柏瑋	弘道國中	41
林冠汝	敦化國中	52	李孝瀅	建德國中	46	郭明錡	東湖國中	44	翁晴	永吉國中	41
吳必穎	興雅國中	51	蕭亞	景興國中	46	邱馨卉	海山國中	43	高延貞	仁愛國中	41
廖書玉	介壽國中	51	林彥誼	自強國中	46	王惟	靜心中學	43	邱志煜	永吉國中	41
林季薇	金華國中	51	呂皓瑋	景興國中	46	陳思瑾	金陵國中	43	李佳薇	建成國中	41
吳駿偉	秀峰國中	51	黃美惠	華興國中	46	張仕杰	明德國中	43	尹文廷	錦和國中	41
張祐寧	士林國中	51	賴柏升	光仁國中	46	周丕晨	士林國中	43	何佳蓉	海山國中	41
陳帛曄	西松國中	51	鄭盺宜	平中學	46	張舒椀	懷生國中	43	周師帆	中山國中	41
余欣叡	弘道國中	51	陳怡帆	瑠公國中	46	和本捷	西松國中	43	趙婉宇	永和國中	41
詹蕙瑜	中正國中	50	洪崇文	萬華國中	46	王鈺茹	江翠國中	43	林乃絹	金陵國中	40
周廷韋	光仁國中	50	陳依辰	中正國中	46	魏鼎	景美國中	43	謝弦舫	師大附中	40
吳亞璇	中正國中	50	黃小綾	民生國中	45	張道原	永和國中	43	鄒念容	介壽國中	40
留逸珊	建成國中	50	蔡若涵	東湖國中	45	柯惠娟	三和國中	43	黃郁惠	景美國中	40
葉晏伶	金華國中	50	傅筱涵	南門國中	45	戴碩甫	海山國中	43	楊家宜	弘道國中	40
陳怡潔	弘道國中	50	陶昌群	仁愛國中	45	林書玉	中正國中	43	洪瑜安	雙園國中	40
余珍媛	仁愛國中	50	蘇意涵	景美國中	45	葉韋廷	興雅國中	43	陳彥如	五常國中	40
陳沛予	景興國中	49	林頎玲	延平國中	45	黃子倫	古亭國中	43	游家慧	埔國中	40
蔡若慈	士林國中	49	蘇怡之	聖心女中	45	謝宛蓉	長安國中	43			

學習補習班‧劉毅英文 (國一、國二、國三、高一、高二、高三班)

國中部：台北市重慶南路一段 10 號 7F（火車站前‧消防隊斜對面）　　☎ (02) 2381-3148‧2331-8822

高中部：台北市許昌街 17 號 6F（壽德大樓）【93 年 1 月份起】

||||||||||||||● 學習出版公司門市部 ●||||||||||||||||||

台北地區：台北市許昌街 10 號 2 樓 TEL：(02)2331-4060・2331-9209
台中地區：台中市綠川東街 32 號 8 樓 23 室
TEL：(04)2223-2838

|||||||||||||||||||||||||||||||||||||||||||||||||||||||||

初級英檢模擬試題 ③

主　　　編／林 銀 姿
發　行　所／學習出版有限公司　　　　☎ (02) 2704-5525
郵 撥 帳 號／0512727-2 學習出版社帳戶
登　記　證／局版台業 *2179* 號
印　刷　所／裕強彩色印刷有限公司
台 北 門 市／台北市許昌街 10 號 2 F　　☎ (02) 2331-4060・2331-9209
台 中 門 市／台中市綠川東街 32 號 8 F 23 室　　☎ (04) 2223-2838
台灣總經銷／紅螞蟻圖書有限公司　　☎ (02) 2795-3656
美國總經銷／Evergreen Book Store　　☎ (818) 2813622
本公司網址　www.learnbook.com.tw
電 子 郵 件　learnbook@learnbook.com.tw

售價：新台幣二百二十元正

2004 年 1 月 1 日一版二刷